DRY AIR ON GANYMEDE

I felt an itching in the back of my throat. My eyes flicked down at the dials mounted beneath my transparent viewscreen. The humidity indicator read zero. I frowned.

Every suit has automatic humidity control. You breathe out water vapor and the sublimator subsystem extracts some of it before passing the revived air back to you. The extra water is vented out the back of the suit. You'd think that if the microprocessor running the subsystem failed, you'd get high humidity.

But I had too little. In fact, none.

I flipped down my rear lightpipe and squinted at my backpack. Water dripped from the lower vent. I checked my—

Dripped? I looked at it again.

That shouldn't happen. The suit should have been venting water slowly, so it vaporized instantly when it reached the extremely thin atmosphere outside. Dripping meant the relief valve was open and all my water had been purged.

D0057605

JUPITER PROJECT

Gregory Benford

BANTAM BOOKS
NEW YORK • TORONTO • LONDON • SYDNEY • AUCKLAND

This edition contains the complete text
of the original hardcover edition.
NOT ONE WORD HAS BEEN OMITTED.

JUPITER PROJECT

A Bantam Spectra Book / published by arrangement with
the author

PRINTING HISTORY
Tom Doherty Associates edition published September 1984
Bantam edition / November 1990

ISBN 0-553-28631-5

Published simultaneously in the United States and Canada

Bantam Books are published by Bantam Books, a division of Bantam Doubleday Dell Publishing Group, Inc. Its trademark, consisting of the words "Bantam Books" and the portrayal of a rooster, is Registered in U.S. Patent and Trademark Office and in other countries. Marca Registrada. Bantam Books, 666 Fifth Avenue, New York, New York 10103.

PRINTED IN THE UNITED STATES OF AMERICA

RAD   0 9 8 7 6 5 4 3 2 1

To James Nelson Benford
. . . who has been there in spirit,
if not in fact.

Father of all! in every age
In every clime ador'd,
By saint, by savage, and by sage,
Jehovah, Jove, or Lord!

—ALEXANDER POPE

Chapter 1

Maybe I should start off with a big, gaudy description. You know—Jupiter's churning pinks and browns, the swirling white ammonia clouds like giant hurricanes, the spinning red spots. That kind of touristy stuff.

Except I don't feel like writing that kind of flowery crap. I'm practical, not poetic. When you're swinging around Jupiter, living meters away from lethal radiation, you stick to facts. You get so vectors and grease seals and hydraulic fittings are more important than pretty views or poetry or maybe even people.

That's always been my trouble—people. The way I see it is, there are always going to be some types you can't get along with. That's something you've got to face. Maybe it's chemistry. Or as the psychers put it, "orthogonal personality constellations." Bullshit, I'd say. But, then, I'm no expert.

I tend to solve my "group dynamics adjustment" problems by going to the low-g gym. Work off the tension. We're supposed to be psychologically in synch out here, with everybody packed into the Can, but even the psychers admit there's always some friction somewhere. I find that working up a good sweat does wonders for my sociability index, and takes the edge off my voice. Not that I'm any great athlete; Matt Bohles will never show up in the Olympics. But at seventeen I wasn't going to turn into a slab of flab, either, even if I did live in a steel box.

So that's how I came to be playing zero-g squash with Yuri Sagdaeff in the first place. I wouldn't search him out for any other reason, that's for sure. I'd never liked him— "orthogonal personality constellation," y'know—and I was pretty sure the feeling was mutual. But up to then we had avoided each other.

Usually I'm pretty easygoing about games. Win some,

1

lose some—it's no big deal. But something told me it was important to win this year's squash tournament. I'd never even come close before, but this time . . . well, something in my subconscious was saying *do it, dummy*. So I was really pushing. I came up against Yuri in the semifinals. I guess that's where all the trouble started.

I was losing.

I couldn't figure it out. Things kept going wrong. Not that I was going to give up, of course. My father says a Bohles isn't really a Bohles if he has the word *quit* in his vocabulary. Dad says it in this kind of cornball way of his, but basically he's right. That's the way I've been brought up. So I dug in and swore at myself under my breath, and got ready for the next point.

But, as I said, I was losing.

Yuri had just served the ball as hard as he could. I watched it carom off the wall of the tube and slam into the forecourt. The squash court is a cylinder, with its top the forecourt wall and the bottom the backcourt—only there isn't any real top and bottom, or up and down, because there isn't any gravity. The object is to bounce a black rubber ball off both ends of the cylinder—forecourt and backcourt—before your opponent can snag the ball with his racket.

I gathered my legs under me, trying to judge how fast that ball was moving and where I could intercept it. I knew it was probably hopeless—that ball was traveling *fast*—and if I missed it Yuri would have me down, 18 to 12.

I clenched my racket and jumped. The hard thing to remember, even after you've been out in space for years, is that in zero gravity just a little push will get you where you're going in a hurry. Sure, your *mind* knows it's true, but your body has to learn it all over again if you've been working in a g-field for a while.

So I overshot.

Too anxious, I guess. I jumped from one side of the tube, about halfway up the cylinder. An instant later I was coasting across, watching that squash ball bouncing back at me from the forecourt, one eye on the ball and the other on the tube wall I was approaching.

It wasn't that the ball was too far away, at all. I could reach it with the racket. But by the time it was within range of the mighty Bohles right arm, I would have to be halfway through my somersault. That tube wall was coming up fast, remember: I had to turn over in midair and get my legs out in front to brake my velocity when I ploughed into it.

I *should* have been able to swat that ball and then flip with plenty of time to spare. If I'd judged it right. Only I hadn't.

"Ah!" I cried, and Yuri laughed at the same time.

Automatically I stretched out my arms to the side and rotated them, to spin me head over heels. Partway into the somersault I had an idea—or maybe just a reflex. Anyway, I flailed around awkwardly with my racket, aiming at a spot behind my back where I knew the ball must be passing.

Thunk! The ball hit the plastic rim of my racket. I finished up my flip and cocked my head around just in time to see the ball drift lazily back into the forecourt, taking its own sweet time.

Then my boots hit the wall and I cushioned to a stop against it. Yuri yelled, started to jump and then thought better of it. The ball bounced softly off the red forecourt wall and came off at an angle. A second later it hit the tube wall and became a dead ball by the rules of the game.

"Tsk," I said mildly. "It looks like you don't get that point after all."

"Luck!" Yuri said darkly.

Yuri pushed off the backcourt wall and glided down to the forecourt. He did a partial repel off the red forecourt and snared the ball, all in one deft movement.

He was good, no doubt about it. He does a lot of no-g work repairing rocket boosters, and he practices. But something was bothering me about this game. I was missing shots I shouldn't have, not getting into position fast enough. And I had a suspicion why.

"Your serve," he said, tossing the ball to me. Yuri is

burly, muscular, and pretty imposing seen up close. He has close-cropped black hair, a square jaw and a squat, flat nose; squint your eyes a bit and he can look like a badly drawn design for a tank.

The tank said to me, "Winded?"

"Hell no! Medical Division has been worrying about you, Yuri, a heart attack, so I thought I'd take it easy on you." Even as I said it I knew it sounded pretty lame, just a lot of phony bravado. It did some good, though—Yuri started turning slightly purple. But then he blinked, as if he were reminding himself that I was razzing him from a position of weakness, and turned away with a grunt.

"Serve, kid."

I decided to try my hunch. I drifted to the back of the cylinder and braked to a stop. Yuri crouched against the wall of the tube midway between the two end walls.

I brought my racket around and served the ball in a diagonal away from him. It hit the forecourt wall with a *spock* and seemed to be traveling pretty fast to me. Yuri pushed off, taking all the time in the world, and swatted the little black ball as it went by him.

Ordinarily, to win the point I'd be turning by this time, windmilling my arms, getting set up for the shot. But I wasn't concerned about the point; I wanted to watch Yuri. One of the tough parts of no-g squash is the fact that maneuvering takes all your attention, usually with your back to your opponent. You can't keep your eye on the ball a lot of the time. So a sort of Gentlemen's Convention has evolved; it says that you should get out of the way between your opponent and the ball, so that when he does get a glance at it he can see.

I maneuvered my shot, not taking any special pains to get into the right position. I watched Yuri out of the corner of my eye. He glided across the tube, looked back at me and kicked off again. This time he followed a line that passed between me and the ball for several seconds, blocking my view of where the ball was bouncing off the tube wall.

I pretended not to notice. I pushed off to my left, opposite the way Yuri was going. The ball came flying out of the forecourt, struck the tube wall and twisted off to the side. Yuri had put spin on it—spin I would've detected if I had seen the ball's first bounce.

I was moving one way and the ball, suddenly, was doing just the opposite, and closing with me all the while. I writhed around, trying to reach the tube wall and get another push, but I wasn't close enough. I made a stab with my racket, but the ball sailed past and *thonked* hollowly against the blue backcourt wall.

"I believe that makes—" Yuri said.

"Nineteen," I finished.

Okay, what he'd done wasn't illegal. It was merely outside the Gentlemen's Convention, and without a referee I couldn't prove it. Now I understood why I'd been missing shots by a few centimeters, having trouble anticipating his moves and losing sight of the ball. Yuri was playing to make that happen.

The next serve was Yuri's. I proved once more that we Bohles are slow learners: Yuri used his same serve, but placed it about a foot further away than usual, so my hit-it-on-the-somersault trick didn't work that time. Besides, I wasn't really concentrating. I was simmering with anger, kicking myself for not noticing Yuri's tactics before.

It was my serve. I took a deep breath; the air smelled sour, flat. I hit the ball viciously, taking out my anger on it, and it came off the forecourt badly aimed. It made a nice, clean setup for Yuri. He hit a quick one past me and I couldn't catch the ball on the rebound. Point to him.

Yuri served, we had a respectable rally that left me winded, and he outfoxed me with a little dink shot to take the game 21 to 13. Game, set, match.

I drifted to a stop in the middle of the court. "Remarkable placement, Yuri," I said mildly. "You must be quite a growing boy, getting bigger every day. It's getting harder and harder to see around you."

Yuri gave me his lummox look. "You imply something?"

"Nothing I can prove."

"Precisely put. Everyone knows I have been practicing to beat you. It would be bad form for you to complain after losing so badly."

"You don't think they'd believe me?"

"Some might wonder . . ." He casually flicked his

racket through the air in a forehand shot, watching it carefully. "But I do not think you are so unwise." He swung again, making a thin whipping sound.

I set my jaw, gripped my own racket . . . and then felt sort of stupid. He was right. I couldn't prove anything, and getting into a brawl on the court wouldn't help.

"Forget it. You have to beat Ishi to win the tournament, and I don't think he'll make the mistakes I did." (I knew he wouldn't. I was going to warn him.)

"Very good." Yuri paused. "I think I shall stay and practice for a bit," he said pointedly.

"Okay, I'm leaving anyway. I'm due on watch in Monitoring."

So I left, feeling depressed. I opened a curved panel in the court wall and wriggled into the one-man transfer pipe beyond. I coasted along it, using every other handhold, and came to another hatch. I went through it into a slightly larger tube big enough for two-way traffic, but I didn't meet anybody in the two hundred yards to the "top" of the center axis.

The squash court, you see, is on the axis of my home. The Jovian Astronautical-Biological Orbital Laboratory, JABOL. Quite a mouthful. We don't call it that, of course—usually it's just the Can.

That's pretty much what it looks like—a big tin can, spinning slowly in the utter black night of deep space. The lid of the Can is a pancake of water, held in shape by a flexible plastic sack. It's a radiation shield, actually. It floats 50 meters above the spinning metal cylinder of the Can. The bottom lid is the same, so you can't look into the Can from outside easily. If you could, you'd see that it isn't solid. There's a big hollow cylinder in the middle, open to space. That's where we store our ships and shuttlecraft. There's room enough, because the hollow center is 200 meters across. And smack in the middle is a long pipe, the central axis, connected by spokes to the main body of the Can. I was in that pipe.

The axis doesn't spin with the rest of the Can; it's suspended on gimbals. That means it doesn't have any centrifugal "gravity"—it's in free fall conditions. Ideal for adapting an Earthside game, like squash, to zero-g.

Don't get the idea that JABOL set the central axis just so for the benefit of squash players—it's all rigged for the Far Eye, our observatory. Over a hundred Can staffers wanted to play the game, and we all had to scrounge the tubing for our court and wangle permission to build it by ourselves, on our own time. It's ours. (Legally, of course, some bureaucrat in the Association for the Advancement of Science back on Earth has supervision—but let him try and use it.)

I reached the end of the central axis. I was still fuming, not thinking about what I was doing, and I almost closed the pressure lock on my thumb. Grimacing, I slipped into one of the personnel transfer tubes. These are the spokes that connect the axis to the Can. I coasted quickly along, ruminating on the game, and feeling the increasing faint tug of centrifugal gravity as I moved outward, radially, toward the rim decks of the Can.

First deck inside the Can is the locker room, complete with 'fresher. I stripped off my shorts and T-shirt, glad there wasn't anybody around to ask me how the game had gone. Under the 'fresher's alternating, stinging showers of ionized water I finally perked up.

Yuri had foxed me neatly, cheating just enough to get away with it. So what? Maybe he'd have beaten me anyway. There wasn't much I could do about it, anyway, right? In future I'd avoid Yuri and that would be the end of it.

Right? Right.
So I thought.

Ten minutes later, all brushed and scrubbed, I stepped out of a drop tube elevator onto A deck, near Monitoring. As soon as the elevator stopped I'd felt a giant's hand on me, the full press of one g, because A deck is the furthest one out from the Can's axis.

I turned left and walked uphill. That's right, uphill. The decks of the Can are cylinders with a common axis, each cylinder fitted inside the next, layered like the skin of an onion. As I strolled along, hands in pockets, five meters below my feet was the outer skin of the Can—and beyond that, the high vacuum of space. I was facing along the rim of the A-deck cylinder, so the floor curved up in front of me, eventually bending out of sight. It always looks like you're walking uphill. You're not, of course, because gravity—the centrifugal force, I call it, though a physicist would shake his head and remind me that it's really "centripetal," according to connoisseurs of mechanics—is perpendicular to the floor everywhere. It never *feels* like you're walking uphill, but it looks that way, both in front and behind you. On the other hand, to right and left the floor stays flat. If the view wasn't blocked by partitions you could see all the way to the "top" and "bottom" of the Can.

The curving hallway outside Monitoring Division is a swirl of yellows and greens that spiral around the doors and splash out onto the deck. All this gives the impression of depth and variety; halls look longer and it's easier for the human eye to locate things, from the contrast. The ship's psychologist says it's good for us—who wants to look at a gray prefab paneling all day?—just like the Ganymede vacations.

In the corridor I saw two women techs pulling some wiring slabs out of a circuitry conduit. Spot-checking a fault, probably. One of them was bent over and, well, let's say my young man's fancy was turned to matters other than electronics. She glanced up and saw me looking. And smiled. I could feel my face reddening. Well, they can't blame you for looking.

I slid aside the door and stepped into the small alcove that led to Monitoring. For some reason my father was standing there, waiting.

"Ah, Matt. Mr. Tsulamba is pulling extra duty today, so you'll go on an hour late." He said this in a straight, informal way, but there was a note of strain in his voice.

"Oh, okay," I said. "I'll have lunch first."

"Got a minute?" he said quickly. He waved toward his office. I nodded and followed him into the cramped little room. Somehow Dad always looks bigger in his office, even though he's only a few centimeters taller than me. The medical people say I'll probably dwarf him in a few more years, since the low-g environment will make all us kids taller. But Dad's over two meters now, without an ounce of fat, and he looks like he wrestles bears for a living. He sat down and put his feet up on his desk—no small trick, in that room—and I folded a straight seat out from the wall to perch on.

"I wanted to talk before you go rushing off to Ganymede. You leave in a day or two, isn't that right?" He frowned, as though thinking to himself.

"Yes, but I'll only be gone a week."

"There are a few things you ought to know before then, and I think you'd better hear them without your mother around." He gave me a wry grin. "Sometimes she takes the edge off what I want to say."

"Uh huh."

He tugged at his long sideburns. "I've been hearing some pretty high quality scuttlebutt. Talk about cutting corners on Lab operations, minimizing expenses—but serious, this time, dead serious. I think there's something behind it. Things are brewing back Earthside. I suspect a few insiders guessed early, several months back. That would explain some of the maneuvering going on in the higher echelons of the Lab." He stared off into space. "In particular, the adroit sidestepping by a certain figure in BioTech . . ."

"You're leaving me behind, Dad. What's happening?"

"Sorry. Let's see—in, ummm, about six months you'll turn eighteen. I suppose you have considered what that means?"

"Sure. I'll be voting age. Only there's nobody to vote for, out here."

He smiled wryly and then frowned. "There's more than that, I'm afraid. Below eighteen, a boy dips into the knowledge and history the human race has accumulated, even though mankind's history is mostly a series of regrettable errors. After eighteen, you've earned the right to make your own mistakes."

"Fine. I'm ready."

"Well . . ." Dad looked uncomfortable. "I have been wondering if you might make your first big mistake if you elect to remain here at the Laboratory."

"Huh? You don't mean I should go *back*?"

"A solid grounding at Caltech will stand you better in the long run than what you can pick up casually here."

"I don't *want* that. For Chrissake—"

"Calm down. Sit." I noticed that I had gotten to my feet without being aware of it. I sat.

"I am only making a few observations," Dad said mildly. "What you do is your business—or will be, six months from now. You are officially a minor until age eighteen. That means you are a member of our family and a student. After that, where you live and what you do is strictly between you and the Laboratory administration."

"Yes," I said. I value my independence as highly as anybody, but it sounded as though Dad was practically throwing me out.

"But you'll always be my son." He smiled. "You know you're welcome in our home. I'm just telling you now, that it's time to start thinking about the future.

"I *have* thought about it. I'm going to stay here," I said, setting my shoulders.

"Now, don't go all stiff-necked on me." He grimaced and scratched his bald spot. "Have you figured out which job slot you're going to apply for?"

"Oh, well, probably for watch officer in Monitoring."

Dad smiled faintly. "I am sure your mother would be happy to know you freely elect to continue working in dear-old-Dad's section. What do you *really* want to do?"

"Uh, something outside, probably. Low-g work."

"Not a bad choice. Just let me give you a little advice. Whatever you want, use the remaining six months to improve your qualifications for the job. I don't believe staying on at the Laboratory is going to be a simple matter for you kids."

"Why?"

"The Project can't support a Laboratory staff that continues to grow. The Earthside administrators agreed to send complete families out here only because they are socially more stable than groups of singles. There were a lot of other arguments—and good ones—against shipping an eight-year-old kid like you off to Jupiter."

"I pulled my weight!" I said indignantly.

"I agree. But some children have to be sent back

when they come of age, or the Can will pop its seams in a few more years. And remember, appropriations for space research have leveled off. Commander Aarons is looking for ways to trim our costs."

"*Some*body will get to stay."

"Certainly, I am merely pointing out that it might not be you."

That worried me. Dad always says that worry is just wasted energy. It wasn't like him to cry wolf.

I glanced at him. He was gazing distantly at a big display screen on the office wall. It showed the placement of all tugs, shuttles and general traffic around the Lab, color-coded in orange and blue according to priority.

"Dad?"

"Yes?"

"I guess you're trying to tell me it's not obvious that I'm supervaluable to the Lab."

"Something like that."

"There are a lot of smart kids about my age. I guess I'd better shift into high gear," I said slowly.

Dad sat upright and looked at me steadily. "The competition is not going to be easy, and you're all trying for the same brass ring," he said seriously.

"Great. I'll give Commander Aarons a demonstration of what I can do," I said grimly. "But what were those rumors you mentioned?"

"Forget them for now. Maybe I can tell you more later. Right now you'd better grab lunch."

"Okay," I said reluctantly.

Dad stood up and handed me a thick pamphlet. "When you have the time, read this."

I looked at the cover. It showed two guys talking earnestly under a tan palm tree. It was a catalog for Caltech.

And *that* unnerved me more than anything he'd said.

Chapter 2

The foldout tables in the rec room were mostly filled, but I saw Jenny Fleming and Zak Palonski at a large table in the corner.

"Can I join the great debate?" I asked Jenny. She smiled and moved over to give me room, straightening the collar on her orange blouse and fiddling with her braids. Yes, braids—pretty unfashionable, back Earthside. Makes her look younger than she is, when everybody knows a mature, mysterious look goes over better Earthside this season. But braids also keep your hair from straying inside a spacesuit helmet.

"My, you do look a little peaked, Matt," Zak said. "I trust you trounced Yuri?" Zak has unruly black hair and is a touch fat. He was rapidly finishing off a plate of goulash.

" 'The vanquished have no tongues,' my son," I said, quoting a line of his own poetry at him.

"Then I must play Yuri for the championship?" I hadn't noticed Ishi Moto was in the cafeteria line behind me; he had come over to the table just in time to hear the news.

"Right. Watch out for—" Then I stopped. Better to tell him later, in private. "—his dink shot. It's subtle. Our last game was a breathtakingly narrow twenty-one to thirteen."

"I shall prepare," Ishi said in a way that implied a lot. Ishi is always calm and it's hard to read that politely expectant look he has. You have the feeling he's sitting back, watching the circus around him with a slightly amused interest, unhurried, enjoying it all. He chuckles at things a lot and there's a bemused twinkle in his eye when he talks.

"Why didn't you challenge me?" Jenny said brightly to me. "I'm out of practice."

"Why?" Zak said. "Working too hard?"

"My shuttle needs some repair," Jenny said. "I've been overhauling it with the help of some people in maintenance."

"Why should that take all your time?" I said.

"It is a long task," Ishi said, "and it must be done as quickly as possible. There are only two shuttles assigned to satellite maintenance. That is the minimum number possible under the safety regulations, since there must always be a backup shuttle in case the first fails while on a mission."

"Yours is still operating, Ishi?" Zak said.

"Yes. I have not been out, though. There have been no malfunctions among the data satellites while Jenny has had the *Ballerina* in the shop."

"*Ballerina*, is it?" I said. "I thought you'd named her *Winged Victory*."

"After that meteorite damage last month, I'm surprised you didn't make it *Victory Winged*," Zak said.

Jenny wrinkled her nose at him and turned to me. "I like *Ballerina* better, and since I was sprucing her up—"

"Fine," I said. "Be sure to change the entry in the Lab log, or twenty years from now a little man in a black suit will come around and ask you to cough up for a misplaced orbital shuttle."

"I know enough to do *that*," Jenny said flatly. She straightened her braids again.

I remembered the sandwich I had made, and dug in. The bread wasn't made from wheat, of course, but some sort of half-breed seaweed that grows better in low-g hydroponics tanks. After nine years I've about convinced myself I like the seaweed better. Almost.

Zak launched himself into a monologue about a poem he was writing, using terms I couldn't follow. Zak is the local Resident Character, junior grade: he's short, intense, and talks faster than most people can think. Faster than he can think, sometimes.

"Hey, Zak," I said through a mouthful of sandwich, "have you thought about sending those poems back to Earth? You know—to build up a following?"

"Ah, sir," he said, pointing a finger at me. "You

reveal your abysmal ignorance of literary economics. Poetry, my friend, is unprofitable. It's not worth the price of a 'gram to tightbeam it to Earth."

"Ummm," Jenny said, "that doesn't sound like the Zak I know. Why write poetry if there's no percentage in it?"

Zak looked shocked, and he was almost a good enough actor to be convincing. "Mademoiselle," he said, "underneath this simple workshirt beats the heart of an artist. You—"

"Your heart is on the left-hand side," Ishi said mildly.

"Oh. Yes. Jenny, you malign—"

"Spare us your sensitivity," I said. "Anyway, Ishi, the human heart is in the middle of the chest. It only sounds like it's beating on the left side."

Jenny leaned across the table—which wasn't hard, considering how small everything is in the rec room—and stared Zak in the eye. "Okay, Zak, I'll accept the assumption that you have nonlarcenous impulses, despite evidence to the contrary. But I've seen you scribbling away in a notebook, and there has got to be money in it somewhere. 'Fess up."

"Oh, you mean my diary," said Zak.

"*Diary?*" Even Ishi was surprised.

"Sure. I've been keeping one ever since I got here, seven years ago." Zak looked around at us, surprised. "You mean you three don't have diaries?"

We all shook our heads. "Why bother?" said Jenny.

"Thou art innocent of the profit motive? Well," Zak said, shaking his head, "I hope you children have someone to lead you around by the hand when you get back to Earth."

"What profit is there in a diary?" Ishi asked.

"Think about it," Zak said, running his finger absent-mindedly around the inside of his milkshake glass and then licking it. "Here we are six hundred million kicks away from Earth, orbiting the biggest planet in the system. The Lab is the farthest outpost of mankind. Don't you think people back on Earth will read an account of life out here, written by—"

"A brilliant young poet?" finished Jenny.

Zak smiled. "Well *I* won't say that. But you never know what a publisher will put in his advertising . . . "

I finished my coffee. "Say, Zak," I said, "have you managed to tear yourself away from your diary to write that script for the skit you're putting on? Deadline's coming up."

"Sure. Almost finished. I'm wondering if there are enough of us to fill all the roles, though."

"Why not expand the cast?" Jenny said.

"Count me out," I said. "I'm playing a guitar solo."

"Spoilsport—say, here's someone you can conscript now. Yuri."

I turned, and Yuri Sagdaeff was sitting down next to me.

"What's all the gab about?" Yuri demanded.

"Are you anything in the next amateur hour?" Jenny asked him.

"Nope. I don't plan to."

"I've got a part in my play that would fit you admirably, Yuri," Zak said.

"Like I said, I don't plan to. I haven't got the time," Yuri said, arranging the food he'd brought with him. He looked at me. "I don't believe you have the time either, Bohles. Not if you're going to ever play better squash."

"I'll struggle along somehow," I said.

"You seem suddenly quite interested in squash," Ishi said. His face was a model of oriental inscrutability.

"I am," Yuri said, taking a mouthful of peas. "I just didn't get around to it before now."

"You were big on chess two months ago, weren't you, Yuri?" Jenny said.

"Sure."

"I didn't know that," Zak said. "I'm a bit rusty, myself. Care to try a game, Yuri?"

"No. I don't play chess anymore."

"What? So soon?" Jenny said.

"You are a man of sudden interests," Ishi said.

"Come on, Yuri, you needn't be afraid of losing to *me*," Zak said.

"It's not the losing. I'm just through with chess."

"Ummm," Jenny said. "Did you finally get out of that trap Mr. Jablons had you in?"

Yuri smiled slightly. "Of course. And I checkmated him in three more moves. That gave me the championship of the Lab."

"Verrry smart, Yuri," Zak said. "Quit while the competition is still looking at your heels."

"You've got me wrong," Yuri said, waving a hand. "I just get bored with the same old thing, is all. Besides, I've got too much work to do. I can't keep up with everything."

"Your group is sending down more probes?" Ishi said.

Yuri nodded earnestly, glad to get the attention off himself. "We're trying to get all the new data we can, in time to be sent back on the *Argosy*."

That's what we were all working toward: the arrival of the *Argosy*, the mammoth ion rocket driven by nuclear power that was our only link with Earth, outside of laser beam. The economics of interplanetary travel are inescapable. It costs a fortune to push a pound of payload from Earth to Jupiter, struggling up out of the gravitational "hole" that the sun makes.

The whole process takes seven months and the *Argosy*'s sister ship *Rambler* follows at the next economical conjunction of Earth and Jupiter, thirteen months later. That means we get a visit every thirteen months. It seems pretty seldom to us, but ISA—the International Space Administration—counts its pennies. We aren't likely to get more.

"Doesn't that put the Atmospheric Studies group ahead of schedule?" Jenny said.

"A little," Yuri admitted. "The series we're planning will just about use up all our liquid oxygen reserves."

"That's not very smart," Zak said.

"Not smart to get no results, either," Yuri said.

"What if some emergency turns up?" Jenny said. "You won't have any high-performance chemical fuel left."

"Wait a minute," I said. "I don't get it. Why—"

"Yuri's talking about those boosters he slaps on the ion rockets that drop our probes into the Jovian atmosphere," Zak said. "You need the boosters when those bathyscaphes start fighting the winds, down there in the clouds."

Jenny pursed her lips. "I still wonder about the wisdom of gobbling up that liquid oxygen."

"Who approved the LOX?" Ishi said politely.

"My father backed it and Aarons went along," Yuri said. "Not that Aarons could've stopped it. My father carries a lot of weight these days."

I was going to ask what he meant by that, but a better idea occurred to me. "Sounds foolhardy to me," I said with deliberate mildness. "Particularly since those bathyscaphes haven't turned up a speck of living matter after years of trying."

Yuri's face tightened. "Look, junior, the day Atmospheric Studies gets a package far enough into the water clouds, below the ammonia layers, that's the day this whole game pays off. *We're* the business end of the Lab. Anything we need, we get first priority."

"My my." I felt my temples throbbing. "I didn't know I was dining with royalty."

"Yuri—" Jenny began in a conciliatory tone.

"Never mind, Jenny," I said, standing up. "I've got better quality guff to listen to. Ishi, you going my way?"

Ishi hesitated a moment and then nodded. "I do have to leave."

"Let's hoof it," I said, and we left the rec room.

We took a drop tube from J deck downward toward A. It was hard to talk while we held onto the conveyor belt loops, so I spent the time figuring how I could've slipped the needle into Yuri better, really gigged him.

We got off at D deck and took a shortcut I knew—in fact, I'd helped assemble that section out of the *Argosy's* leftover fuel storage drums years before. We kids get used for low-g work a lot, because we seem to have better reflexes—and what else could we do out here, anyway, without a goldplated PhD?

"You seemed tense back there, Matt," Ishi interrupted my thoughts. "You wanted me to leave with you. Is there something—?"

So I told him about Yuri's squash tactics. Ishi seemed to already know half of what I said; very little gets by him on any level, however subtle. When I was through Ishi nodded and said mildly that he would deal with Yuri when the time came. I chuckled inwardly, thinking with relish about Yuri's impending doom. Ishi would do something crafty but completely fair, absolutely above board—and I'd enjoy every delicious moment of it. Then Ishi said, "You seem more disturbed by this than I would expect Matt. Is there something about Yuri that bothers you?"

An idea flickered across my mind and I suppressed it. "He's an oaf, that's all."

"You reacted as though threatened by him."

"He—he tries to intimidate me, lord it over me."

"Yuri is a type, that is all. There are many of them in the world."

"Not in *this* world, not in the Can," I said fiercely. "He's a type I can do without. I heard through the grapevine that he waited until Mr. Jablons had a heavy work schedule in the low temperature lab. Then Yuri challenged him for the chess championship."

"Ah. So Mr. Jablons did not have free time to think over the game between sessions? Ummm."

I was glad I'd gotten Ishi off the subject of me and onto Yuri. And Monitoring was nearby, so I mumbled a farewell and ducked down a side corridor. I thumbed through the Caltech booklet to keep busy; there were a lot of 3Ds showing crashing white surf, rugged gray mountains and orange groves. What they didn't show was the press of people, the pollution, the gang fights in the streets. They didn't tell you it was a dog-eat-dog world back there, a zoo with all the animals out of their cages.

I stepped into the small alcove just inside the doorway of Monitoring. There was nobody there, so I dimmed the lights and went through a side door into the Main Station Room—only nobody calls it that, naturally; it's known locally as the Hole.

An apt name, too, because it's utterly dark. I stood for a moment and let my eyes adjust, not daring to move. After a while I could see the dim red lamps spaced evenly between the booths. My booth was the fifth down and I moved toward it at a slow shuffle, being careful not to bump into anything.

The Hole isn't very big—no larger than a decent-sized apartment—but it's crammed with equipment. I could hear someone murmuring from around a corner in the aisle; that meant the required minimum of one man on duty was satisfied. But the voice was just a drone, relaying some numbers to the bridge, so there wasn't anything urgent.

I slipped into my booth and my hands fitted automatically into the control slots. I logged in and tried a few practice commands: a view of Europa, Jupiter's second moon, off the port bow (reddish, ridge-streaked, most of it eaten by shadow); the docking area, from two separate cameras, showing three men maneuvering a storage drum into place; a shot of free space, with an orange rim of Jupiter in one corner. I switched over to radar.

Then I got down to business. I was sitting in my own separate booth, with my view completely filled by a soft green screen. It looked very much like an old-fashioned radar screen, with one important difference: the blips of detected objects show in three dimensions, since it's a holographic projection. I could see a jumble of stuff in the center—the Can itself and things parked near it. Then, farther out, were tiny points of light that constantly shifted and changed, vectoring in an elaborate dance.

Every second the pattern changed. Jupiter is a huge, massive planet, with a swarm of junk orbiting around it. The solar system's asteroid belt lies between Mars and Jupiter; Jove has captured a kind of asteroid belt of its own. Compare Earth: it has Luna, a few pint-sized rocks, and that's all. Jupiter has thirty-nine moons, three larger than Luna, and enough garbage orbiting it to make a half dozen more. Most of the junk wasn't discovered until the first expedition came out this way, and it's been a nuisance ever since.

I punched a few buttons and, in mathematical language, asked the ballistic computer a few questions. The machine blotted out a small rectangle in my screen and printed its answers:

NO IMMINENT COLLISIONS RECORDED.

UNKNOWN OBJECT NOTED 13:45 HOURS. PRELIMINARY CALCULATION INDICATES NO DANGER.

YOU ARE SECOND WATCH OFFICER.

I relaxed. There wasn't going to be much to do on

this watch. The chunks of rock and ice that revolve around Jupiter are dangerous—they can zip through the Can in a thousandth of a second, depressurize a level and kill somebody before it's patched. But there weren't any of respectable size headed for us.

Still, I checked out the unknown that had appeared at 13:45 hours. Its orbit showed that it was following an ellipse that crossed over the northern pole of Jupiter. The interesting thing was that the orbit swept right into the upper reaches of Jupiter's atmosphere—so close that, after a few passes, it would plunge in and burn up from sheer friction. That was unusual. Most of Jupiter's "asteroid belt" circles around it in the ecliptic plane, far out from Jupiter's rings and the big moons. This was a good-sized lump, too; radar showed it to be bigger than the Can itself.

Anyway, it was no danger to us. Possibly it had come in from interstellar space just a few days ago. Or maybe it was just an eccentric bit of matter from the asteroid belt. The computer would store the data, and someday a research student back on Earth would use it in a study of the solar system. That's one of the reasons we—the Jupiter Project—are out there.

The computer nudged me: INVENTORY DUE.

I'd been dawdling, musing about that stray chunk of rock. I thumbed a button and the screen erased. Another button, and I was looking at a set of concentric red circles. The center circle was shaded yellow; it represented Jupiter. Each ring around Jupiter was a survey satellite. Most of them were in close to the top of Jupiter's atmosphere, orbiting just above the clouds of ammonia. Ammonia is the same stuff used in household cleaners, only in Jove's chilly upper atmosphere it's frozen into little crystals.

I went through the inventory, typing out questions for the computer about each satellite. Some were recharging their batteries from sunlight right now and transmitting engineering data. Others were bleeding off the excess charge they'd accumulated from particles in Jupiter's radiation belts, so they weren't working at full power. I had to check all these things and be sure the operation was "normal" for that particular satellite.

Routine work, but necessary. We get a lot of vital information from the satellites, and they're the only way we have of knowing what goes on close to Jupiter. The Can itself is a million kilometers farther out.

This time I cleared my board right away. If a satellite had shown a malfunction, though, I'd have to carefully diagnose the trouble and turn the problem over to Jenny or Ishi. A sick satellite is no joke. Whoever was on duty would have to make a house call on the patient and fix the thing on the fly, in free space.

I thought about that, absentmindedly tapping the console keys. I like working in Monitoring, sure, but it didn't exactly make my blood sing. With only thirty teen-agers in the Can, Commander Aarons has made an Eleventh Commandment that we fill in where needed. So my personal preferences hadn't mattered when they moved me indoors, off the repair gang, and into Monitoring.

But I wanted to be *working*, dammit, using my hands. I could maneuver shuttles and skimmers and one-man jetters—but here I sat on my ass, a clerk.

I grimaced and glanced over at the Caltech catalog. Inside, outside, Earthside—where was I going?

Chapter 3

Zak called me just before I went off shift. He and Ishi were fooling around with nothing much to do. "C'mon over to my place and we'll goof off," Zak said. I had some time free, so I went.

Zak and Ishi were back in Zak's tiny bunkroom, wedged in like sardines. Zak's parents weren't home yet and Zak was messing around with the computer terminal he had installed next to his bunk. "Hey, close the door," Ishi called to me.

"You kidding?" I replied. "The three of us packed in here'll bring on claustrophobia fits."

"We want some privacy, Matt old man," Zak said mysteriously.

So I closed the door and perched on the edge of Zak's bunk. "For what?"

"This," Ishi said, with his usual eloquence. He flicked on the big display flatscreen on the wall. A black and white picture formed out of a pearly background fog. A woman. Pretty, with long legs. She was peering off to the left. She wore a flowing robe.

"Who's she?" I asked.

"A creation of mine," Zak said.

"A snip from Earthside 3D?" I asked.

"Well, that's how she got started, yeah. You remember me telling you about those new Simulife codes I got?"

"Sure. For taking a mechanical system and studying the stresses. You start off with a new design for a grappling arm, say, and the computer draws a picture of it for you. Then you give it jobs to do and the computer studies how the thing will move and what strains it will take. You can see the grappler making awkward motions, and then redesign it to avoid that. It's—" I noticed the two of them grinning at me. "Hey . . ." I said, thinking.

"You are a quick student," Ishi said wryly. "Show him, Zak."

Zak punched a read-in code. The woman began to move. She stood up. She smiled right at us and I guess she was about twenty, maybe twenty-five. She had a nice smile. She was still staring toward me as she reached up and her fingers found a clasp at her throat. The robe fell. She wasn't wearing anything under it. She was, well, spectacular.

"Damn," was all I could say.

"I can tap in for color," Zak said, and her skin became a rosy tan. Green eyes. Dark black hair, so black it seemed to have traces of blue in it. She began to turn slowly. A little mechanically, I thought. But then I, ah, got more interested in the general effect, and she didn't seem so awkward anymore.

"And 3D," Ishi prompted.

"Check," Zak's fingers talked to the central computer some more and the woman changed from a flat image to one with perspective. Fully rounded, yeah. She had a special luxuriant look about her that . . . well, bigger and better than life, is the way to put it, I guess. She was certainly better than anything I'd ever seen in the Can. It suddenly struck me that the images of women I'd been seeing in 3D for years were always more spectacular than the women and girls I saw in everyday life. False advertising, sort of.

"Zak, you've got a good thing here," I said. "You've surpassed yourself."

Ishi grinned broadly. "Matt, you lack imagination."

Zak typed in for a routine he'd obviously set up beforehand. "I call her Rebecca," he said mildly.

Rebecca began to dance. She was good. She jiggled in all the right places and I followed her movements intently. It was hard to believe a program designed to test out how machines would function, before they were ever built, could do *this*. Zak had taken Rebecca off some 3D show and fed her specs into the programming, and here she was, sexy as hell.

Then a man walked on stage.

He was naked. And he was visibly interested in Rebecca. Very visibly.

Zak snickered when he saw the expression on my face. "Here we go, boys."

Zak had imagination, that was for sure. He'd named the guy Isaac. Isaac was big and burly and had been around the world. Rebecca was entranced by him. Anything Isaac wanted, he got. They did it in the regular old Missionary Position, and then in a chair, and then standing up. We three sat there and watched. Nobody said anything, even though I knew this wasn't new to Zak or Ishi. They were still too interested, though, to make any wisecracks. Some things you don't get tired of so fast, I guess. And me . . . well, for me a lot of it was new. Sure, I'd seen the manuals, and gone to the Becoming An Adult 3D courses they imported from Earth, and all that stuff. But to *see* it . . . that was something else.

"What'll you have next, gents?" Zak asked. Isaac and Rebecca were still going at it in the middle of the screen. Each of them was staring at the other with fixed smiles. I wondered if it was the mechanical programming or whether people were really like that when they, well, Did It. I had no way of knowing, of course. "Uh . . ." I began, and stopped. I knew my face was turning red again, but there didn't seem to be anything to do about it. Rebecca and Isaac went on with their relentless energy. I knew there was a certain rhythm you were supposed to hit; the books all talked about it that way. The books had spoken about techniques and methods . . .

"Geez, Matt," Zak said, "you look like you're doing your homework."

Ishi chuckled. I realized I'd been dodging the whole thing by concentrating on the technical points. "Well, maybe that's the way I am," I growled.

"C'mon, relax," Zak said. He tapped his console. Rebecca and Isaac jerked and moved. They got into a new position. Then they were at it again. Bam, bam, bam.

"Kind of repetitious, isn't it?" I murmured.

"You should've been here a couple of hours ago," Ishi said. "Ol' Zak here had them going at it like rabbits. Double the speed, Zak."

He did. We all burst out laughing.

"Not a very dignified act, is it?" I commented.

"Dignified, schmignified," Zak said. "It's the real stuff."

"No, it's just a sim."

"I didn't notice you falling asleep."

"Okay, okay, it's pretty good. In fact, damned good."

Ishi asked idly, "I wonder if that's what those porno movies are like?"

Zak nodded. "That's what gave me the idea."

"To duplicate pornos?"

"Sure. Commander Aarons isn't going to let that kind of thing come in over the 3D tightbeam. But if we can make them *here* . . ."

I started to see it. "Ah. You're going to sell tapes of your talented Rebecca?"

"I don't see why not."

I slapped my brow. "Zak the flak. Geez, you'll do *any*-thing for money."

Zak said airily, "Ideas have a momentum of their own, Matt-o. That's one of the lessons of history."

"They'll nail you. They'll uncover it in the memory files."

He arched his eyebrows. "You imagine I would overlook such a vital facet of the problem? I see you have inadequate respect for the jewel-like clarity of my mind."

"Okay, okay, what's your out?"

"I have a storage place they'll never find. Absolutely safe."

"Where?" Ishi asked.

"Come now. Professional secret."

"So you work out a whole set of pornos," I said, "and then sell the index code, so kids can tap into it?"

"There will be a random resorting of the index, of course, from time to time. To keep the customers from giving the information away. Only I will know the basic location."

Ishi said, "Free enterprise, he calls it."

"Look, somebody's got to do *some*thing to liven it up around here."

I smiled. "So you think there'll be a big market for your machine-made porno movies?"

"Why not? The stuff we get from Earthside is all oatmeal puree. Entertainment for all the family. *Bor*ing."

"So you figure to sell them to everybody?"

Zak shook his head. "Why would adults want them? Hell, they've got all the sex they need."

Ishi laughed. "I think you're a little naive about your marketing strategy, Zak."

"Oh, yeah? Wouldn't *you* lay out some coin of the realm to see ol' Rebecca doing her thing?"

Ishi nodded. "Maybe. But it would have to be really good."

"Look, you guys," Zak said energetically, "let's cut the crap. We all know the Can is a tightly run ship, in more ways than one. Here we are, nearly eighteen years old, and not a single one of us has gotten laid. Right?"

"Right," I said sourly.

"That means there's a lot of repressed impulses floating around."

"Which you'll make a buck out of."

"Well . . . maybe. I'll tell you one thing, this move of

mine has made me think about our tight little tribe here. They give us all these up-to-date courses and we have social mixers and all that, sure. But the plain fact is that we live in each other's hip pockets. There's no privacy. Your family is always just around the corner."

Ishi said, "Like some incredibly small town."

"Check. You know how in schools back Earthside, they give you an essay to write on what you did on your summer vacation?"

"Yeah."

"Well, what everybody knows is that if you're older than fourteen, you spend your summer vacation trying to get laid. And if you're lucky, you make it.

"You score," Ishi said.

"You mean," I said, "by the time kids Earthside are our age, they're . . ."

"Right, they're men of the world, compared to us."

"You think so?"

"I *know* so. Novels and movies are all about that. For Chrissake, it's a major theme!"

Ishi chuckled. "You've got a point."

"I think I know why, too. I mean, why we're so stifled up here."

"That's easy," I said. "We're busy. It's dangerous out there. Maybe you've noticed."

"That's a piece of it, yeah," Zak said. "I did a little researching, though, and turned up a study. *Sexual Suppression in Closed Communities*, it was called. It turns out that in places like the Israeli kibbutzim, nobody gets laid either, unless they're married. There's a thing called 'outgroup bonding' that forms. Like an incest taboo, almost. You get to feeling you can't have sex or romance with a member of the group you grew up with. The pressure is always on you to defend against some threat, so you get in the habit of thinking about girls as if they're allies. Not, y'know, potential lovers."

"You think that explains it?" Ishi asked.

"Sure. Hell, the author of the study gave the Can as an *example*. She said we'll probably work out the same way as the kibbutzim. I think that's why the study was done in the first place—to find out what to expect out here."

"Ummm," I murmured. "I dunno . . . "

"Say, Ishi, I just remembered something."

"Oh?"

"When I mentioned that nobody got laid around here, you kept quiet."

"So I did."

"You mean . . ."

Ishi smiled faintly. "I cannot lie to you. But I will give no details."

Zak and I glanced at each other. For Chrissakes, *Ishi*, of all people! He seemed so reserved, so quiet, so— "You never gave any sign," I said. "Y'know I used to notice that when Zak here would be swapping dirty jokes with me, you never said anything. I thought you were shy."

"Maybe he had a more direct approach to the problem," Zak said.

"Ummm . . ." I studied Ishi's mysterious smile. Suddenly I felt like a punk kid. And back Earthside, all of us kids would probably look like social throwbacks. Sex was a big part of growing up and we hadn't even started on it yet. But Ishi had.

I said, "How'd you find a girl you would . . . you know . . . ?"

Zak said, "In that magic phrase, Do It?"

"Uh, yeah."

Ishi pursed his lips. "It is the way you ask the question which tells the true story, Matt."

"Huh?"

"Here in the Can, we are very careful to keep orderly behavior. So the society tends to use the social forms that were current when our parents were growing up. There has been a tradition of seeing the relationships of boys and girls as a contest."

"Yeah," Zak agreed. "They're supposed to hold out on you, and you try to talk 'em into it."

"Come on, it's not that bad," I said.

"Oh yeah?" Zak said sarcastically.

Ishi said mildly, "There is some truth in Zak's words. But as well, our parents wish to protect us. Without thinking of it in so many words, they try to keep us children. It is difficult for them to see us as nearly adults."

"Yeah, so to keep from dealing with our sex lives, they arrange it so we don't have any," Zak said.

"Let us say it is easier for them if they do not have to handle such delicate matters."

Zak said, "Technical types are kind of shy anyway. They sweep the subject under the rug."

"We don't *have* rugs in the Can," I said. "But look, you guys make it sound like some kind of conspiracy."

"Quite so, it is not," Ishi murmured. "We are speaking here of an unconscious pattern. There are Marxist economic theories for this separation and anger between the sexes, of course. I have read them. But I do not think they truly explain matters."

"The fact remains, Ishi, that you know a girl who is reachable," Zak put in.

"Yeah," I said, eyeing Ishi. He only smiled. The unspoken point was that a girl who would Do It for Ishi might Do It for one of us, too. I mean, it's not a pretty idea, but that's what I was thinking. I was pretty sure Zak was, too. In fact, Zak might have stage-managed this whole conversation to find out if Ishi or I knew any good candidates. He's shrewd, ol' Zak is. Not shrewd enough to solve the Getting Laid Problem, though. And even I could see we were thinking about this the same old way, with girls as half-enemy, half-ally, but, well, that's the way the world *was*.

Zak insisted, "You know a girl that we know, too, who—"

"Correct," Ishi said, grinning.

"C'mon, who is she?"

"I'll say no more, Zak."

"Look, we won't tell. We just want to know—"

"I'm not going to say."

"Geez, at least you could tell us what it was *like*. I mean, is it—"

"I have told enough." Ishi said it in a soft, even voice, and I could tell he meant it.

After that, nothing much more happened. Ishi put up

with our grousing. He wouldn't give away any more information about the mysterious Lady X who'd lifted the burden of virginity from his shoulders. Zak told a seemingly endless series of dirty jokes. I wondered if adults spent this much time on the subject and decided no, that was impossible. When you can *do,* you don't talk.

Zak's mother came in from her job in Physical Chem. She peered in at us, all scrunched together, and gave us a curious look. Zak hurried to erase the encoding for energetic Rebecca's program. After that we joked around a little, the way you do, and then when there wasn't anything more to say, I went home.

Chapter 4

The tubeway lights were dimming as I walked home. The air pressure was dropping too, I knew, though the change was so slight I couldn't feel it. The Can is more than metal walls and oxy bottles; it has to ebb and flow like a natural environment, to fill the human need for a rhythm, a cycle. It has some decidedly non-Earthside benefits, too, like the low-g sleeping dormitory, where you can get the equivalent of a full night's sleep in about four hours. The way I felt, maybe I'd be using the dormitory tonight.

When I slid the door aside, though, my father was sitting in his favorite chair, reading a fax sheet, and there was a toasty, cooking smell in the air. Troubles seemed far away.

"What's on?" I called out.

"Salad, artichokes, veal, custard," my mother said quietly, coming out of the small kitchen and wiping her hands on her apron. "And please do not shout at home."

"He was only releasing a little tension," Dad said. "He had to sit through one of my lectures today."

"Oh?" Mom said, instantly concerned. "About—?"

"Yes," Dad said. Evidently they had talked over my future before broaching the subject to me.

"Well, you needn't be so glum," Mom said. "The two of you look as though Matt was shipping for Earthside tomorrow."

"Well, I am shipping for Ganymede in two days," I said, making a try at changing the subject.

"I know, and we'll miss you," Mom said. "I don't see why we don't take our recreation trips together, when—"

"Leyetta," Dad said. "A nearly grown boy doesn't want his parents tagging along after him wherever he goes. We're sandwiched into a small enough area as it is."

"Hmmm," she said noncommittally, and went back into the kitchen. "Dinner is almost ready."

I used the time to stow my schoolwork, straighten up my room and wash my hands. One of the troubles with living in the Can is the squeeze on space. My bedroom is about as big as a decent-sized closet on Earth. I have to keep it neat and put everything away in the wall drawers or I'd go crazy. I'm told we were all tested to find whether we were naturally orderly, before we qualified for the Jupiter Project. No slobs allowed. How they decided the eight-year-old Bohles brat was okay I can't guess, but they did.

"Matt," my father called, reminding me that I may have learned to be neat but I'm not always on time.

Dinner was good, as usual. Dad presided over the serving of portions and I dug in. I didn't pay much attention to the small talk about events around the Lab until Mom said:

"I heard an interesting rumor today, Paul. The *Argosy* leaves in a week or two, doesn't it?"

"Yes, it must. That's when the optimum conjunction comes up for the Earth-Jupiter cruise."

"Well, one of the women who works in Hydroponics with me heard that Earthside asked for a personnel inventory several months ago," Mom said.

"Surely they have that information already," Dad said.

"No, they wanted a new assessment of everyone in

the Laboratory. And that's not all. Earthside asked if there were any jobs that weren't getting done because we don't have the time."

"ISA thinks we're shorthanded?" I said.

"I don't believe the International Space Administration 'thinks' anything," Dad said. "It is too large, like a dinosaur, to do anything more than stay alive. The higher functions are left for others."

"Oh, Paul," Mom said, and looked at him with an amused smile.

"Well, perhaps I overstated my case. ISA takes orders from the Association for the Advancement of Science, and somewhere in that anthill a few people decide what happens and what doesn't."

"Mom, do you think ISA will send us some more staff members?"

"I don't know, I just work here. But that is what the rumor seems to imply."

"Just a while ago Dad was warning me that ISA might ship a lot of us kids home when we reach eighteen," I said.

"I will admit that does not seem to agree with the rumors," Mom said.

"Ah," Dad said, raising a finger. "There are several ways to interpret that. If ISA does send you back, Matt, they will have to replace you. The work must be done by somebody."

"I wish you hadn't thought of that," I said.

"I'm merely guessing, son. A word of advice: don't waste your time trying to fit one rumor against another. Everyone in the Lab knows there is some sort of administrative battle going on in ISA and that there may be changes in our work here. An atmosphere like that breeds rumors faster than your mother can grow this veal in her tanks."

I took another mouthful, thinking.

"If ISA is going to send us more staff, I would like to know about it," Mom said. "We will need the time to increase our farming cycle."

"Dad," I said during a pause in the conversation,

"why is all this happening? Why is ISA rocking the boat now, after the Lab has been out here nine years?"

My father made a tent with his fingers and leaned over the red-topped table. "Like most human problems, it is a matter of too many things happening at once. Earth is running out of raw materials. The fossil fuels, like coal and oil and natural gas, are going. Those don't hurt so much, because we have thermonuclear fusion to provide all the power we want. Fusion reactors drive the *Argosy* and the *Rambler* and run that electric light, there." He pointed at the ceiling lamp.

"But once the oil is gone, what do factories use for lubricants? Where is the lode of iron? There simply isn't any."

"We're mining the asteroids," I said. "It's not like we're living during the Breakdown, in 1990 or—"

"Sure, that's a help. In fact, without it Earth would have to cut back drastically and go without a lot of things."

"It's that serious?" Mom said.

"I am afraid it is. We have been isolated out here. Any outpost of humanity has a tendency to think of news from home as rather unreal, after a while. I have been following the news summaries sent out from Earth and it looks to me as though things are pretty bad. That Canadian war didn't help."

Mom frowned and tugged at her red hair. I suppose Dad hadn't mentioned any of this to her either, before now.

"Look, Dad," I said. "The asteroid mines are paying the way for the space program. Why should ISA's budget problems affect us?"

Dad smiled ruefully. "We knew when we signed on with the Jupiter Project that this Lab was the poor relation of the asteroid program—right, Leyetta?" Mom nodded. "Well, it seems to me things have gotten worse. ISA knows very well it can get metals and rare minerals out of the asteroids. But what can they get out of us?"

"Why, why—lots of things!" I sputtered. "We're finding out about Jupiter, the biggest planet in the system."

"Give that young man a silver dollar—asteroid silver, of course."

"Huh? Isn't scientific research worth paying for?" I said.

"Matt, dear," Mom said, "I think you are underestimating the importance of boredom in human history." With that she got up and began clearing the table. I helped her in my usual style, balancing a saucer on a glass on a plate.

"Your mother speaks like the Delphic oracle," Dad said, "but she is, as ever, correct. All those intelligent citizens back on Earth aren't paying for knowledge. They want romance, adventure—vicariously, of course."

"Adventure?" I said, putting the dishes into the electrostatic cleaner. "Out here?"

"Adventure is someone else doing something dangerous far away," Mom said. "The Jupiter Project qualifies on all counts."

"Aw, it's not so dangerous."

"Oh?" Dad said. He had gotten out a deck of cards and the cribbage board and was setting up for our standard three-handed game. "Here we sit, surrounded by the radiation from Jupiter's Van Allen belts, in absolute cold, high vacuum, far from the sun, the nearest help seven months away at best, without even a planet beneath our feet."

"Okay, it's a little dangerous. But so is crossing a city street."

"Getting hit by a commuter bus is ordinary, Matt," Mom said, "but a meteorite is another matter."

"Precisely. The trouble is that we've been pretty careful out here and nothing very exciting ever happens. That lets out the adventure part. The only thing left is romance."

"Romance," I said thinking. "Oh, you mean hunting around for alien life forms."

"Yes," Mom said. She was straightening up the kitchen and making out a list of groceries to request for tomorrow. There isn't much storage space so she has to plan ahead every day. She flicked on our stereo and light, mellow music flowed into the room and covered the faint noises from other apartments. She looked up at me. "Your father is something of a pessimist about Man as a political animal. But I do agree with him that the man in the street back home cares only about the chances of finding life on Jupiter, dear, no matter what else the Laboratory can do for science."

"The only trouble is—woe is us—the Lab has not been able to find life," Dad said. "I suspect the taxpayer and ISA both are getting tired of waiting."

I spent a moment sorting out the leftover food from our plates and putting it into the disposal tube. Thirty seconds later it would begin a new career as recycled fertilizer in Hydroponics.

"What bothers me most about this damned business," Dad went on, "is that some people in the Lab have known about ISA's doubts for months now. A couple of department heads kept their ears to the ground. They've been trying to use that information to enhance their own careers—"

He stopped abruptly. One of Dad's cardinal rules is, no talk about Lab infighting. Gossip is what people turn to when they run out of good conversation. I can remember him saying that there's no harm in having nothing to say—just try not to say it out loud.

And Dad had started to violate one of his own rules. It meant he must be more worried than I thought.

Mom put an arm around me and said, "Come on, you two. That's enough. Politics inhibits the reasoning processes."

"Correct. Cribbage!" Dad said with a new energy. "Sharpens the mind, lightens the soul. You're three games down, Matt, as I remember. Leyetta, your deal."

The next morning I spent with Mr. Jablons—the one who lost the chess game to Yuri—learning electronics in his low-temperature laboratory. A lot of our instruction is on a one-to-one basis, by necessity.

Take me, for example. I like electronics. I spent more than a year, back when I was twelve years old, building electronic detectors for our satellites. Kids are pretty good at small handwork like that, if you can get them to sit still long enough to get the job done. My specialty was a little beauty called a Faraday Cup. It measures the total number of charged particles that strike a satellite. They have to be built just right, or they're worthless.

But after all, how many kids are interested in Faraday Cups? When I was learning about them Jenny was maneuvering skimmers and Zak was talking to computers. I comprised a class of one.

That's the way I like it, too. Big classrooms with thirty kids crammed in, listening to an adult yak for an hour—well, you can keep it. That sort of education went out with the twentieth century and nobody misses it. I've heard they're trying something like it again, though, back on Earth, because the taxpayers have started squawking about the costs of teaching programs. It's just one more thing to make me glad I'm in the Jupiter Project.

When Mr. Jablons was satisfied that I understood the new circuitry he'd explained, he left me alone. I built a simple blackbox arrangement, incorporating the new circuit, as an exercise. It filtered radio signals and passed one narrow band of wave-lengths. I tried it out by listening in to some of the routine signals coming from our observation satellites near Jupiter, and the darn thing actually worked. I congratulated myself and walked down to the Education Center.

I was supposed to put in some time on a teaching machine, brushing up on differential equations. Instead I hung around outside, reading the bulletin board, until Jenny turned up.

"Say, I thought you were logged for teaching machine time now," she said.

I made a face. "That's just what I need, a girl who'll nag me until I straighten up."

Jenny tossed her head, sending her brown braids tumbling in the low gravity. "I wasn't aware that you needed any kind of girl at all." She gave me a fierce snarl. I made a demon face back at her.

"Attention!" the loudspeaker system said. Heads turned in the corridor.

"I have an announcement," a deep voice said. It was Commander Aarons'. "The *Argosy* has been delayed in its departure from Earth orbit. A series of holdups in fueling her and a few unexpected repairs will make it necessary to

reschedule her usual cruise. ISA informs me that the
Argosy will be delayed at least two weeks. This will result
in the *Argosy* reaching us about two and a half weeks after
her scheduled arrival. Section and Division leaders should
alter their work programs accordingly."

The loudspeaker went dead with a click. I looked at
Jenny. "What does that mean?" she asked.

I shrugged. "Not much. We'll have a little longer to
get our reports ready."

"Why bother to announce it? There's a thirteen month
wait between ships anyway. What difference does a few
weeks make?"

"Come on, dummy. There's a favorable configuration
between Earth and Jupiter that opens every thirteen
months. If the *Argosy* misses it, the trip gets a hell of a lot
more expensive."

"How much more? I mean, if ISA is worried about
budget—"

"Come on." I gestured toward one of the study quads.
"We can probably find out from computer retrieval. *Argosy*
was slated for the minimum-energy orbit, so if it's late . . ."
I started figuring in my head.

Zak came strolling over. "Hear the news?" he said.

We nodded.

"I took the trouble to run a calculation, since I was
using a teaching machine at the time. If the *Argosy* is
delayed more than four weeks she won't make it within
budget."

"Rather close," another voice said. Yuri had moved in
quietly to a position close beside Jenny.

"I wonder if ISA has anything up their sleeves," Zak
mused.

"Impossible to say. Anyway," I said, glancing at Yuri,
"it's not our job to worry about ISA. Better we should find
something new to dazzle the folks back home."

"Was that crack directed to me?" Yuri said sharply.

Jenny said quickly, "I don't think Matt—"

"What if it was?" I said casually.

"You ought to get your facts straight before you open
your trap, Bohles," Yuri said.

"What facts?"

"The fact that Atmospheric Studies works harder than anybody else in this Lab. The fact that we've run more probes into the upper atmosphere of Jupiter than the original plans called for. The—"

"Spare me the advertisement," I said.

Yuri took a deep breath and was about to say something when Zak broke in. "Look, Yuri, we all know those things. ISA is starting to wonder why, with all this work, the Lab hasn't turned up any evidence for life somewhere down in that ammonia atmosphere. I guess it's natural for the rest of us—the ones who don't work in Atmospheric Studies—to wonder, too."

"There isn't any answer, no matter what people like Bohles think," Yuri said, jutting out his jaw.

"Okay," I said, "give us a hard one."

"I *would* like to hear about it," Jenny said, turning on a brilliant smile.

So Yuri launched into a song and dance about the incredible hardships his group worked under, and how his father in BioTech was shouldering a staggering, superhuman work load—well, that was the implication, anyway. He gave us a lot of facts and figures to go with it, and those were interesting stuff, the straight scoop. As I listened it dawned on me that Yuri was going to be stiff competition for a staff position in the Lab. Commander Aarons and the others were going to be weighing him against me . . .

I focused my attention back on the conversation. Yuri was describing their latest descent, the one that malfunctioned from pressure overload.

"Meaning, it got squeezed to death," Zak put in.

"—before it could report on its experiments to find life. But the package of instruments did show that deep in the methane and ammonia there is water and it is warm, as warm as this room is now. All the conditions necessary for life are satisfied."

"Then why haven't you found any?" Jenny asked innocently.

Yuri pressed his lips together. "We don't know."

"Yuri, you help put together the rockets that drop

instrument packages into Jupiter. It's not your fault if they don't turn up anything," Jenny said comfortingly.

"Right," Zak murmured.

"What puzzles me is that your probes go deeper and deeper, until the pressure crushes them, and they still don't find any living matter. No airborne spores, no bacteria, nothing," I said.

"We'll fine some, Bohles," Yuri said, with a sudden flash of anger. "Just give me elbow room. You will see results." And with that he got up and left the room.

"Well, all this outdoorsy stuff didn't calm *him* down any," Zak said. "So much for the healing effects of bird songs."

"Yeah," I murmured, "he was going along fine for a while there. I guess we just reminded him of his problems and he covered up his worries by getting mad at us."

"Pretty deep analysis, doctor," Zak said.

"Go on, you two," Jenny said. She got up and palmed the room lights down, and then left.

"I cast off for Ganymede tomorrow," I said, "should do me good to get away from Yuri."

"You can count me in as well," Zak said.

"You're going?"

"I don't much want to, but the psych people say I should," Zak shrugged.

We watched Jenny walk down the corridor and out of sight. Skirts are even more impractical in low gravity than they are on Earth—harder to keep from creeping up, for one thing—so everybody wears pants. But there's no way to disguise a woman when she wants to be noticed, and Jenny departing was far more pleasant and interesting a view than the fake countryside of the meeting room.

"I think she's a little miffed that her peacemaker attempt between you and Yuri fell flat. She'll be okay by tonight."

"Sure. See you at 1900 hours? Got to go practice my guitar."

1900 hours meant a small party at Ishi's apartment. Ishi's parents maintain as much of the traditional Japanese life as they can, living 390 million miles from Nippon.

They sit cross-legged on the floor, on tatami mats, and have delicately shaded woodblock prints on their walls. In the air hangs a faint background smell of rice and the salt tang of fish. It all blends together into a warm feeling of home.

Zak, Jenny, and I sat in Buddha position and took part in the ancient tea ceremony, exchanging small talk with Ishi and his parents. (My back ached, but I like the mild green tea.) Ishi didn't seem bothered by the speculation over sending us Earthside. But then, nothing ever seems to disturb Ishi.

I didn't mention his Lady X to him, even though I sort of wanted to. I didn't have any specific questions in mind, but still . . . The best way I can explain it is that Ishi had *been there*, and I hadn't. And it really was true, what Zak said about how a kid should spend his summer vacation trying to get laid.

It was a quiet evening. After the party broke up I walked Jenny home. Making our way through the hushed corridors, with only the whirr of the air circulators. I noticed that I did feel kind of uneasy with Jenny. She was more like a buddy to me than a, well, a woman. Females have a clear moment when they change from girls to women, at least in the biological sense. Males don't have that. I wondered if it explained some of the way I was feeling. Boys had no way to tell they were men. I mean, nobody pinned a badge on you or anything. So maybe in the back of our heads all the guys I knew in the Can were still boys, without that magic touch. Getting Laid was for sure one signpost, though. There just didn't seem to be any easy way to do it. Society sure as hell didn't help. And the whole damned business seemed so irrational, too. Why should I keep feeling that odd, diffused affection for Jenny? Maybe Zak's kibbutzim analogy was right after all.

Anyway, when we stopped outside her door, I leaned over and kissed her. The idea seemed to go over. She put her arms around my neck and the ol' pulse rate picked up a bit. But then she let go and smiled and stepped back and murmured something nice and that was it. I made a grin I could tell looked awkward and foolish.

I felt confused on the way home. I wasn't very good

at figuring out the swirl of emotions I had inside me. But then I shrugged. *Forget it*, I told myself. Concentrate on the problem in front of you; that's always a good rule. Take 'em one at a time. In the morning I was bound for Ganymede, the fourth moon of Jupiter. I forgot about Jenny and Zak and Ishi and Rebecca the passionate, and went on home to get some sleep.

Chapter 5

We assembled near the axis of the Can, already suited up. All Laboratory vehicles, from the small one-man shuttles Jenny and Ishi used, to the ion cruiser used on the Ganymede run, are kept in the center of the Can.

As I said before, the Can is a big rotating drum. Most of that drum is empty. The middle of the Can, except for the axial cylinder and the connecting spokes, is open to free space. Our cruiser was parked there and we had to go out and board her.

Captain Vandez stood at the air lock, checking over each of us to be sure we had all our suit vents closed, hadn't put our helmets on backwards, or something equally stupid. It's in the regs; he has to do it. A technician who never goes outside can forget a lot in the nine months between mandatory "vacations" on Ganymede. Anything overlooked in free space can be fatal.

"Sing out when I call your name," the Captain shouted. "Williams! Kandisi! Bohles!"

I answered and turned to look at the rest of the party. Zak waved from the other side of the tube, where he was holding onto an inset ladder. We were in very light gravity, almost at the axis. Orange signs reading ANCHOR YOUR LIFELINE—ALWAYS! jumped out at you from the white walls.

"Sagdaeff!"

Yuri answered. "Yo!" I twisted around; he was ten meters behind me. I had a funny empty feeling.

In a moment Captain Vandez said, "You have been on this milk run before, so I will not make a big speech about being careful. Remember, the *Sagan* is an ordinary cruiser. She's adequately shielded against high energy particles but we can't carry the mass to stop big chunks of rock, or even little ones. That means everybody stays in their suits, with helmets in place and ready to seal, *always*. Anybody violating the rules will have to deal directly with me, and that can be unpleasant. All right, into the lock!"

We filed in. We were exiting through one of the personnel locks and there were handholds everywhere. I felt a thrumming vibration through the soles of my suit as the pumps sucked the air out of the crowded lock. My suit limbered up and my arms and legs became easier to move. I read the meters and colored displays set below the edge of my viewplate, to be sure my suit was feeding air properly, balancing my temperature and perspiration, etc. The air tasted a little oily, but then, it always does. There are some things engineering never does get around to solving.

The vibration stopped, a red light winked over to green above the big door, and the outer hatch came free. Captain Vandez pushed it open himself. He gestured at a silvery thread fastened to the edge of the lock. It snaked away beyond view. The fellow in front of me leaned forward and snagged it. He climbed along it, hand over hand.

I was next. I clamped a sliding fastener to the line and cast off gently from the lock with a kick.

Every time you go out, it hits you hard. I was coasting along toward the "top" of the Can. The "lid" was pulled aside, to let the *Sagan* out. It looked like I was gliding toward an ocean of stars, down a bright metal tube. The safety line ended by a lock in the side of a spiderlike fusion cruiser, the *Sagan*. She was moored near the very top of the Can, against the awesome backdrop of stars.

The thing I like best about open space is the feeling

of complete, utter freedom. It's as if I was a bird, able to fly straight and true.

Part of all this poetry comes from the feeling of weightlessness. Zero-g is pleasant enough inside the Can, but out here there's a sensation of freewheeling liberty. It's like having a weight lifted from your shoulders that you hadn't even known you were carrying. I felt great.

The man ahead of me had reached the cruiser. I watched as the *Sagan* grew, and I tumbled over just in time to brake my impact. I felt a touch proud of the maneuver, it proved that freefall squash had kept my zero-g reflexes in shape.

I slipped carefully into the *Sagan's* lock. The inner hatch was open. I pulled myself through and found myself in a long room with passenger seating arranged completely around the walls. A man in a ship's officer's suit gestured to a seat and I sat down. I clipped my thigh fasteners to the seat and waited.

The cylinder was filling rapidly. Our luggage had been brought aboard earlier—they didn't want people trying to carry cases while they negotiated their way across to the *Sagan*.

Zak came aboard and clipped in next to me. I noticed he was already eating some of the food rations recessed in his helmet. I hoped I never felt that hungry: the rations are balanced for nutrition and high protein, but they come out of squeeze tubes, and I've never been able to get over the feeling that I'm eating toothpaste.

After a while everyone was in and the lock closed. I felt a tug of acceleration as the *Sagan* nosed out of its mooring point and drifted free of the Can. There wasn't any way to see this, of course: the passenger cabin was just a concession to us poor cattle and doesn't have any viewing screens.

There wasn't any cheerful speech by Captain Vandez, either, about our destination and flying time and how soon we could expect to be touching down on Ganymede. This isn't a commercial airline. Instead, after some nudging back and forth by the attitude jets, I felt a sudden kick in the stomach. At least, that's what it feels like when you aren't ready for it. The *Sagan* was accelerating away from

Jupiter at about one g. For the first minute or so it felt decidedly uncomfortable. Then my body remembered where it was born and accepted one g as normal; my muscles relaxed a little and my breathing leveled out.

The odd thing about the *Sagan*—or any fusion rocket craft—is the silence. I guess I've watched too many old-time movies about the adventures of Captain Daring, Space Explorer. In those the rockets always take off with a roar like a lion with a hotfoot. The ship throws flame and sparks everywhere. Captain Daring clenches his teeth as the vibration shakes him, and you would swear that a hydrogen bomb couldn't make more of a racket.

Maybe it was like that, once. Now, out in free space, chemical rockets are as outdated as the horse. We use them to brake atmospheric probes as they fall into Jupiter, but that's because they're a one-time only item. Those little one-way jobs are the only ones I know that we use chemical rockets for nowadays. The days of Captain Daring and his thundering jets are gone.

Still, they might be an improvement over the dead quiet way the *Sagan* takes off. There's something kind of creepy about smoothly gliding away from the Can, with no sendoff at all.

Zak tells me I'm a romantic. Maybe so. Or maybe I just watch more old movies than he does.

After the acceleration leveled off I leaned my helmet against Zak's. "Want to see the view?"

He nodded. I got up and pushed off toward the front of the passengers' compartment. Captain Vandez hadn't started spinup or pressurized the ship yet. I met an officer just coming in the hatch and touched helmets with him.

"Okay if we go forward and watch over a 3D?"

"Well, Ah suppose so. How many a you? Jest two? Go on, then. Grab a handhold, mind, don't jest float around. Nevah know when somethin' might up an' happen."

I waved to Zak and wriggled through the hatch. The next compartment was half-filled with baggage and secured in netting. We were in the inner tube that ran down the axis of the *Sagan*. Around us on all sides were storage tanks. At the moment the tanks were empty; the *Sagan* was returning to Ganymede for more water.

Against the walls were several 3D screens. These were the only concessions to the passengers, aside from seats, that the *Sagan* made. The screens gave front, rear, and several side views. In color.

Zak bumped into me, but I ignored him. I was busy trying to estimate our trajectory. The rear view was the interesting one.

No, "interesting" isn't the right word. Beautiful is more like it. In the center of the screen, directly behind the *Sagan*, was Jupiter.

Jupiter. King of the ancient gods. Lord of the Romans. The lion. The giant. The fat man. Jove.

It filled the screen, striped with horizontal bands of yellowish-brown. The bands churn like thick smoke, each band revolving at different velocities. At the equator the swirling clouds go around Jupiter in just under ten hours.

That's what they are: clouds. We've never seen the surface of Jupiter, the solid rock and metallic hydrogen, and we never will. We can't get there. The pressure at the surface is thousands of times larger than the pressure at sea level on Earth. We could never design a ship to go there. Even if we could, there's nothing to see by. No light. The clouds I was looking at absorb nearly all the sun's light, or reflect it back into space.

I strained my eyes, looking at the equator. I could just make out the writhing masses of giant clouds as they boiled over each other, racing around the planet. Below the ammonia clouds I could see were thousands of klicks of methane crystals, hydrogen, ice, sulfur fumes, thunderclaps, and lightning storms as big as the continent of Asia— a cauldron of instant death for any man who went there.

The lion: Jove contains seventy percent of all matter in our solar system, outside the sun. Even this far out, it filled the sky. Down below the equator churned the Red Spot. A swirling awesome storm, bigger than a dozen Earths. Each of Jupiter's bands is a deep layer of gas, spinning at its own speed as the planet whirls. Each has its own grainy, gaudy texture. Here and there a fat storm filled a whole band, rolling like a ball bearing between the bands above and below. Yellow-green lightning forked between purpling clouds.

"Ahem!" A woman cleared her throat next to my ear. "I don't think you boys should have the first look at everything."

"We got here first," Zak said reasonably.

"Rushed up here before we had barely gotten under way, you mean," the woman said, pushing in front of us at the rear viewscreen. She was as old as my mother and not half as good looking.

Zak opened his mouth to say something and I muttered, "Come on, it's not worth it. We've got all day."

We moved over to the forward viewscreen.

"Are you boys going to block *everything*?"

"We're watching—" I said.

"Well, really, I think you should be grateful your parents even let you go on this trip alone. If you can't keep your manners—"

"Our parents haven't got anything to do with it," Zak said. "It's Laboratory regs, once we're above sixteen."

"Humf! We'll see what the Captain thinks about two young—"

"Oh, forget it," I said. "Come on, Zak." I didn't know the woman. She must have come in on the *Rambler's* last flight.

On my way back to my seat I noticed the air pressure building and popped my helmet seal. I cocked my helmet back and sat down, wondering what I was going to do until we touched down on Ganymede.

Zak went in search of something to read; all our study materials were in our luggage. He came back with two chips of Earthside magazines.

I clicked one in my LCD and read at random. One article was about the staggered working hours in the cities and how much it unsnarls the traffic tie-ups. There was a 3D picture of the subway "packers" of New York—men hired to shove people into the already crowded subway cars, so they can carry a few more. That one earned a double take.

The next article I read was a fashion tip for men: Handy Hints to Get the Right Tint. It had a 3D of a man wearing a maroon coat with an ascot, painting his fingernails.

I asked Zak if he thought Commander Aarons edited the copy that came through the laser beam from Earth.

"Why should he?"

"Well, it seems to me Earth comes off pretty badly in these magazines," I said. "I mean, I'd almost suspect somebody was trying to keep us from getting homesick."

Zak put aside his poetry magazine. "Just what is it—oh, I see. Painting fingernails is for women, right?"

"Yes."

"Who says so?"

"Why—well, *my* father doesn't do it. Neither does yours."

"Yes, they are rather conservative, aren't they? After all, Matt, the Lab is a backwater. An anomaly."

"How do you mean that?"

"We've got something to do, out here. You follow little green blips in Monitoring. I talk to computers—everybody's got a job. Even that brat back there—" he gestured behind us, where a baby was yowling—"will have something to do in a few years. Cleaning out the scum in the hydroponics tanks, I hope."

"So? They have work on Earth, too."

"That's where you're wrong." He pointed a professorial finger at me. "They've got jobs, yes. The government sees to that. Plenty of them. But there's not much work."

"You lost me again."

"How would you feel if you had to sit in an office every day, passing pieces of paper from one cubbyhole to another?"

"Bored, I guess. It would be like going to one of their schools all day."

"Probably so. It makes you feel pretty useless. That's the point. People like to see their work *doing* something; they want to see a final product. A chair, maybe, or a bridge, or a 3D."

"Uh huh."

"But that's all done by machines. The men just push buttons and move paper around."

"And paint their fingernails," I said scornfully.

"Sure. Because they're *bored.* They're not doing anything they think is significant. Oh sure, the government *says* paper-passing is productive labor, but there's so much make-work people know it's a sham. That doesn't jibe with their ego, their self-image."

"Uh-ho, here we go again."

"Okay, I'll skip the jargon. The point is, they're trying to show their individuality and worth through something other than their work. It's like birds displaying colored feathers."

"Expressing themselves."

"Right. Only, out here, we've really got something to do. Fads don't catch on here. We're a different culture, really. You wouldn't look down on a Fiji islander just because he wasn't wearing a Brooks Brothers suit, would you?"

"No, but—"

"Anyway, Commander Aarons doesn't have time to worry about what you read," Zak said triumphantly.

I was still trying to straighten out that jump in the subject when Yuri came clumping over.

"Have you thought about what you are going to do in your recreation time?" he said.

"Sure," Zak said. "Just what we usually do—stay away from the crowd."

"Crowd?" Yuri said, his thick forehead wrinkling.

"That's what we're out here for, lummox," I said. "To get away from metal walls and people."

"I usually try to get in shape. You know, run a few klicks and play some volleyball."

"Fine. Go ahead," I said.

"What else is there?" he persisted.

"I usually go out in one of the Walkers. The men at the base are always happy to get some help," Zak said.

"Same for me," I said.

"What for?" Yuri asked.

"My friend," Zak said, "you are no doubt aware of the Ganymede atmosphere project? The base there spends most of its time building new fusion plants, to generate power. The power is used to break down the rocks into basic carbon compounds, water, and oxygen. They're slowly building up an atmosphere that we can breathe. Only, it's a complicated business. They need to know how the air and the temperature is changing all over Ganymede, not merely around the dispersed fusion plants."

"So they've put out recorders and pocket laboratories, all over Ganymede," I said. "Every now and then somebody has to go out and collect the data or make a repair."

"It's a fairly dull job if you happen to live on Ganymede all the time," Zak said. "A tour of the ice fields can get monotonous. But to people like us, it's a chance to get out and see things. So I volunteer, every recreation period."

"I see," Yuri said. "You little squirts are always into something, aren't you? Me, I'm going to stick to my athletics. It might come in handy." He looked at me significantly.

"See you around," I said. Yuri took the hint and walked away. I went back to my magazine.

Chapter 6

It was a long flight. Ganymede isn't any further away from Jupiter than the Can—in fact, the two are in exactly the same orbit. But not at the same *place* in that orbit—the Can tags along after Ganymede, a million kilometers behind.

Sure, it would be easier to study Jupiter from an orbit closer in; near one of the smaller moons, like Io, say. But Jupiter's radiation belts are too intense there, so we have to watch Jove from a safe distance. Even so, the Can still needs those pancake "lids" of water to screen out the hard radiation that sleets in on us. We got the water from Ganymede's ice fields. Ganymede is our corner grocery store out here; anything we can't mine out of its crust has to be boosted all the way from Earth.

Ganymede is so vital to us, I once got the idea that maybe we should move the Can, put it into orbit around Ganymede itself. Make ourselves into a sort of a moon around a moon, so to speak. My father sat me down and drew me some diagrams, and showed me that Ganymede would block out a lot of our transmissions to Earth, not to mention the telemetry from our satellites near Jupiter.

And its reflected light would interfere with our telescopes. So the Can trails along behind Ganymede at a position called the Trojan Point, where its orbit is stable. And every flight between the two takes over eleven hours.

So I was dog tired when we got there. The *Sagan* makes few concessions to passengers; I was sore from my space suit and restless from doing nothing.

Most of our party was asleep when the blue and brown disk of Ganymede rolled into view in the forward port. Zak and I sneaked up to get a better look, even though the seat-belt light was on. I passed Yuri dozing in an aisle seat, no doubt reliving his triumph at squash. Well, I thought, he still had to play Ishi. I ignored him.

But he tripped me as I went by.

I stumbled slightly in the weak gravity and heard his hollow chuckle. "Still clumsy, eh Bohles?"

I knotted my fists and started to say something.

"Oh, mama's boy is taking offense?" Yuri interrupted me. "Tsk tsk."

"C'mon, Matt," Zak said, putting a restraining hand on my shoulder. "Don't bother."

I didn't say anything. There was nothing I *could* say that wouldn't come out sounding like I was whining. After a pause I turned and followed Zak down the aisle, seething. We looked out the forward viewpoint.

Blue ice and frost spread out from both poles of Ganymede. Around the equator was a thick belt of bare brown rock and river valleys. The rivers sliced through the rims of ancient craters. The valleys were choked with a pale ruddy fog; naked peaks jutted about it.

Thin atmosphere sang around the *Sagan* and we went back to our seats. In a moment our nose bit in and we settled into the long glide down.

We were here for two weeks of frolic away from cares, away from family, away from the Jovian Astronautical-Biological Orbital Laboratory. The family part is important: the psychers say it's good for kids like us to get away from the *loco parentis* every half year. Keeps down the nervous wigglies in the Lab, makes it easier to live all together in one huge tin Can.

There was a sudden tug as Captain Vandez gunned

her, a faint dropping sensation, and then a solid bump. I started unstrapping.

Zak snapped shut his book of poems—brushing up on the competition, he called it—and patted around for his glasses. With them on he looks like the kid computer ace he is; when he's in his literary lion phase he pretends he doesn't need them.

"Collect youah baggage on the ground," came a shout over my suit radio. I motioned to Zak and we were the first ones into the air lock. It cycled and the hatch popped open.

I stared out at a range of steep hills, covered in white water frost. About five hundred meters away I could see the slight gray tinge that was the life dome, against a sky of black.

"Move it!" someone called over radio. I looked down and saw a man waving at the drop rope that hung by the air lock.

"Over you go, kid," I heard Yuri's voice behind me and somebody kicked me out into space. I grabbed for the rope, caught it with one hand. In Ganymede's one-third *g* you don't fall fast but I was still recovering when I hit the ground with a solid thump.

I took a few steps away from the rope and then turned back. Yuri was just finishing a smooth slide down.

"You're still clubfooted, junior," he said and I took a swipe at him. He dodged and it landed on his shoulder.

"Come on," I said, setting my feet.

"Mad about a little roughhousing, smartass?" he said with mock surprise.

Somebody shoved me aside. I turned threateningly and saw it was the man who had secured the drop rope. "Break it up!" he snarled at me. "Get out of the way of the rope. You kids can play big men somewhere else."

Yuri walked away. I tried to cool off and waited until Zak came down.

"He's still riding you, huh?" he said.

"Looks like it."

"Yuri hates you being brighter and quicker than he is. So he uses muscle instead. Don't let him provoke you."

I balled up a fist. "I'd like to—"

"Yeah, I know, But that's playing his game."

"So what? I can't—"

"Listen, he's got you going both ways. That guy didn't see Yuri boot you out, he just heard you try to pick a fight. So Yuri got all the points in that scramble. Listen, next time just treat him okay. Maybe after this he'll feel square with you."

"Well . . . maybe."

A winch was already lowering nets of baggage from the cargo lock. We walked over and helped two men unroll the net. Our cases were in it. We scooped them up and started toward the base buildings. They housed some of the fifty permanent staff members; the rest lived under the life dome, farther away.

The *Sagan's* jet splash had melted the ground and made a brown spot in the ghostly white. We trotted along, my suit chuffing away to fight off the cold. When the first expedition landed here the surface was at 150 degrees Centigrade below zero. The reclamation project has warmed things up, but not much.

We reached the administration building and banged on the lock. In a moment the green light winked on and we cycled through. We came out in a suiting-up room. I popped my helmet pressure and found the air was sweeter than I'd expected; they're making improvements in the base all the time. We lugged our bags into the next room and found a man behind a counter with a clipboard.

"Your name—oh, Palonski and Bohles. Welcome back. Gluttons for punishment, aren't you? I see you asked for a Walker again."

"Better than refueling duty," I said and he chuckled. Pumping water and ammonia into the *Sagan's* tanks is the most boring job imaginable: you watch dials for two hours, spend five minutes switching hoses, and then sit two hours again.

He assigned us bunk numbers and let us go; the families with children would get a complete lecture on safety and a long list of things they couldn't do. I'd heard the lecture ten times before and could probably give it about as well as he could.

We found our bunks and stowed our gear without wasting any time. We didn't want the mob to catch up with us. As soon as things were squared away Zak and I beat it across the base and trotted over to the dome lock.

The dome is the whole point of Ganymede, for me. I was out of my suit and putting on tennis shoes almost before the air lock had stopped wheezing. I had to gulp a few times to adjust my inner ear to the dome's pressure, but that was automatic. Anybody who has been in space learns to do that without thinking—or ends up with lancing ear pains when he forgets. Zak was just as fast, and we went through the door together.

To anybody living on Earth I guess the dome wouldn't be a big deal. But to me—I came out the door and just stood there, sopping it up. Overhead the dome arches away, supported by the air I was breathing. It rises to 500 meters in height and is five kilometers in diameter; a giant life-filled blister on Ganymede. Inside the blister is the only spot where a man can walk without a suit.

Zak and I trotted the klick to the ski shed. There is a funny nose-shaped hill under the dome, with one steep face and one shallow. We carried our skis up the difficult side and strapped them on. I stood looking out, surveying the land under the dome. Hills sloped into each other, making stream beds and narrow valleys. A late morning water fog rose from a marshland. Up near the top of the dome, so thin you had to have faith to see it, was a wisp of pearly cloud. Back at the edge, the way we had come, a few people were spreading out from the lock.

"Come on!" I said, and pushed off. We started slowly and then began to weave, making long undulating patterns down the hill face. You don't get as much speed in a lighter gravity, but you can make incredible turns and prolong the ride.

We skied most of the afternoon, until there were too many on the slope. Then we took a hike around the dome to see what was new. The experimental farm had grown and most of the crops—adapted corn, root vegetables, apples—were doing well. The farm is the seed of what Ganymede will become, once the atmosphere project gets going, melting dirty ice to make air.

With the greenhouse effect warming things up and microorganisms giving off oxygen, eventually a soybean will grow somewhere and then—well, then colonists will be panting down our necks, wanting to get in. By then it will be time to push on . . . before they build a Hilton.

That is, assuming ISA didn't send me back on the *Argosy*, I reminded myself.

That thought wasn't so easy to brush aside. I tried pretty hard, though, the next two days. I climbed hills, skied and played soccer until my legs threatened to stop holding me up. When we got up in the morning Zak would just lie in bed groaning about his past sins, and wish for a chocolate sundae to tide him over until breakfast.

The third day we were skiing sort of halfheartedly, waiting for enough people to show up to make a soccer team, when I lost sight of Zak on the slope.

I turned uphill, came to a halt and looked around. There was nobody very near. I poled my clumsy way uphill and looked again. There was a small mound nearby. I skirted around it to get a better view.

"Hey!" Zak said. He was lying in a small depression behind the mound. His skis were off and there was a brown gouge in the snow.

"Why didn't you yell before?" I said, clomping over to him.

"I was embarrassed. It's kind of dumb to take a fall on an easy grade like this." He grinned sheepishly.

"Hurt anything?" I put out a hand to help him up.

"I don't think—*ow!*"

"Sit back down. Let's see." I unwrapped his left ankle.

"How is it?" He blinked owlishly at his leg.

"Sprained ankle." I started unclipping my skis.

"Will I be able to play the piano again, doctor?"

"Sure, with your feet, just like before. Come on." I got him up and leaning on me. "Think you can walk?"

"Certain—*ow!*"

He did make it, though, to the bottom of the hill. From there I hiked back to the dome lock and got a small wagon usually used to haul things to the experimental farm. The base doctor walked back with me and bandaged up Zak's ankle, making the same diagnosis I had, only using longer words.

I got him settled into his bunk. The doctor delegated

me to bring him his meals and the first thing Zak asked for was a milkshake. I shrugged and went over to the cafeteria to weasel one out of the cook—no mean feat.

I asked the man tending counter and he told me it would be a few minutes—several people had lunch coming up. I stood aside to wait. The woman from the *Sagan* was next in line behind me. She asked for a cup of coffee and a vegetable roll and got it immediately. Then she leaned over to the counterman and said loudly, "These youngsters all want special favors, don't they?"

I stood there trying to think of something to say until she flounced out. If it had been Zak, he would have come up with something cutting and brilliant, but I acted as though I had a mouth full of marbles, and my face burned with embarrassment.

"You're the younger Bohles, aren't you?" a deep voice said.

I looked up. It was Captain Vandez; he looked tired. "Yes, sir."

"I heard about the Palonski boy just now. Unfortunate."

"It isn't anything major," I said. "Zak will be walking by the time we ship home."

"Good." He nodded abruptly. "The base commander has you two slated to take the Walker out on a routine inspection tour starting tomorrow. I was afraid this accident might scrub it."

"It will."

"Not necessarily. Another boy volunteered for the job two days ago. I told him both places were filled, but now there is a spot vacant. You see, Bohles, base personnel are all assigned to other jobs now and we are a bit squeezed. If you don't mind going out with another boy . . . "

"Who is he?"

Captain Vandez sighed and looked at a paper in his hand. "Sagdaeff. Yuri Sagdaeff."

"Oh." I gulped. "Could I let you know in a few minutes?"

"Of course. Take your time."

I got the milkshake and put it in a sealed carrying box. I was still in my suit, so I put on my helmet and cycled through the cafeteria lock as fast as I could. Then I double-timed it through a low-lying pink haze back to our dorm.

When I told him Zak stopped slurping and made a raucous noise.

"That sneak!"

"Huh?"

"Remember when we told him about the Walker? I know just how his mind works. Sagdaeff thinks we're making points by doing the inspection tour. He wants his share."

"What for?"

"Yuri wants to rack up points with Captain Vandez and hope the words get back to Commander Aarons about what a sharp guy our Yuri is. He's not dumb."

"Aren't you being a little cynical?"

"Every realist is at first called a cynic," he pontificated.

"You don't think I should go?"

"You're just giving him a break. After all, you and I have been out in the Walker before, doing odd jobs. The guys here at the base *know* you're not a Johnny-come-lately."

"The work has to be done," I said firmly. "The project is more important—"

"Okay, okay," Zak said, rolling his eyes. "Go ahead. Tramp the icy wastes with Yuri for the glory of the ISA. I'll stay here and write terrible things about you in my diary and starve to death."

I gritted my teeth, thinking. I was nervous and jittery. A small voice was nagging me in the back of my mind. *Don't be a sucker*, it said. It had some good arguments, too.

But I knew, finally, what was right. So I went back to Vandez and volunteered again.

"Look, we can't *all* be like you," I said to Zak, later.

"Uh huh."

Zak wanted me to go out and see if any girls were around the base, just in case we'd missed any. To amuse him while I was gone, he said. "Didn't you bring your tapes?" I asked him. "Just conjure up ol' Rebecca. She'll keep you delighted."

"Don't knock her, kid," he said, smiling cynically. "She'll make me a buck yet."

"Uh huh," I said, and went to sleep.

I woke up that night, sweating.

The dream had come back again. I'd thought it was gone for good, but no—my pajamas were soaked, my heart pounding, I was breathing in short, desperate gasps.

And I was in that sun-bleached Costa Mesa schoolyard again. The two Chicano kids had backed me up against a wall. They were elaborately casual, chewing gum, sneaking amused looks at each other.

"Smart kid, aren't ya" the biggest one said. He put his hand on my chest and gave me a light shove. I stepped back to keep my balance.

My lip trembled. "I'm not slow, if that's what you mean."

The big one looked over at his friend. "They always got somethin' ta say. Little smartasses."

The second kid punched me in the shoulder. I moved back and felt the rough brick wall behind me. There were more Chicano kids behind these two now; a crowd was gathering.

"He's gonna fly off into space, too," the big one said to the crowd. "Too good for us *compres* down here in the mud."

"I don't see any mud here," I said. My voice sounded weak and distant. "Just dust."

The big one whirled around, fists clenched, face reddening. "You're always right, ain't cha, kid? Mebbe you oughtta *taste* dust."

He hit me in the face. I felt something break in my nose. Somebody punched me in the side. Suddenly everybody was shouting. I tried to take a swing at someone, anyone. The big kid cuffed my fist aside and slapped me again, laughing. There was a buzzing in my ears.

I tried to run. Something struck me in the stomach and I stumbled, reaching out. The crowd was all around me. They were thick and close and everywhere I turned arms pushed me away. They spun me around in a circle, taunting me, calling names.

I struck out blindly. I was crying, begging them, throwing punches in a red mist that smothered me. I heard them jeering. Something smashed me hard in the stomach. I went down.

The noise washed over me. Somebody kicked me and I felt a sudden stab of pain in my ribs. The dust clogged my nose. I choked.

The world seemed to blur and drift away. I grunted, clawing at the dirt, and rolled over. The jeering was a hollow echo, an animal chorus.

I felt a wetness on my lips. I licked at it, thinking my nose was bleeding. I felt a spattering on my face. Somewhere kids were laughing, jeering.

I licked my broken lips again. Then I caught it: the warm, acrid smell. The stench of urine . . .

"Matt! Hey, what's the matter?" Zak was shaking me.

I realized I must have been moaning, half-awake. I gulped and deliberately slowed my breathing. "An old nightmare."

"Must be pretty bad," Zak said sympathetically.

At that moment I really needed a friend. So I told him about it. I'd never mentioned it before, even to my parents. But this time it was worse than ever before. I felt as if I had to tell somebody.

"Wow," Zak said when I was finished. "That happened just before your family was selected for the Project?"

"It's my last clear memory of Earth. I was eight."

"The nightmare keeps coming back, huh? That explains a lot."

"Explains what?"

"You're known all over the Can as a monomaniac, a hustler. Working is your *life*, Matt. The psychers make you take time off, like the rest of us, sure. But even here on Ganymede—you were the one who got me into the Walker business, check? You're always looking for a job, some way to distinguish yourself."

"Well, of course," I said irritably. "What's wrong with that?"

"Nothing, nothing at all. But with you, it's a mania. You've *got* to succeed."

"Uh, maybe . . ." I began to feel uncomfortable.

"Because if you *don't*, you won't become a JABOL staff member." Zak paused, thoughtful. "You'll be shipped Earthside. Back into that schoolyard in—southern California, wasn't it?—with that zoo of welfare refugees. The heat, the dust, the big guys picking on you . . ."

"Aw, crap. Stop playing Young Freud."

"You don't see it, do you? Ever wonder why you get so tense and irritable with Yuri?"

"Because he's a bastard!"

Zak stared at me. "A big bastard, too, isn't he? Lots bigger than you. A big kid," he mused.

"Get this," I said intensely, "that guy doesn't scare me. It's only sometimes . . . sometimes I get mad." I paused for a moment. I didn't want to talk about this any more.

"Look, I've got to get some sleep," I mumbled.

"Okay," Zak said noncommittally.

I rolled over, face down into my pillow. Zak clicked off the light.

But I didn't get much sleep that night.

The next morning I suited up and walked through the scattered buildings that make up the Ganymede base. The Walker was parked at the edge of the base; its mate was off on some other task.

It stood on six legs and was six meters tall. The living quarters were in the bubble set on top. The bubble had big, curved windows facing in all directions, with an extra large one set in front of the driver's seat. Beneath it, almost lost in a jumble of hydraulic valves and rocker arms, was the entrance ladder.

The Walker was painted bright blue for contrast against the reddish-brown dirty ice of Ganymede. The antenna on top was green, for some reason I have never understood. Underneath the forward antenna snout was neatly printed *Perambulatin' Puss*. Everybody called her the Cat.

"Morning!" I recognized Captain Vandez's voice even over suit radio. He and Yuri walked up to the Cat from the other side of the base. I said hello. Yuri made a little mock salute at me.

"Well, you boys should be able to handle her," Captain Vandez said. He slapped the side of the Cat. "The ole *Puss* will take good care of you as long as you treat her right. Replenish your air and water reserves at *every* way station—do not try to skip one and push on to the next, because you won't make it. If you fill up at a station and then go to sleep, be sure to top off the tanks before you leave; even sleeping uses up air. And no funny business—stick to the route and make your radio contacts back here sharp on the hour."

"Sir?"

"Yes, Bohles."

"It seems to me I've had more experience with the Walker than Yuri, here, so—"

"Well, more experience, yes. You have taken her out before. But Sagdaeff practiced all yesterday afternoon with her and I have been quite impressed with his ability. He is older than you, Bohles. I think you should follow his advice when any question comes up," he said impatiently.

I didn't say anything. I didn't like it, but I didn't say anything.

Captain Vandez didn't notice my deliberate silence. He clapped us both on the back, in turn, and handed Yuri a sealed case. "Here are your marching orders. Follow the maps and keep your eyes open. Good luck!"

With that he turned and hurried back toward the base. He was a busy man with a lot to do. I supposed I shouldn't be too mad if he relied on the older of us two—usually, the kid who has been around a while longer can handle himself better. It was just that in this case I disagreed.

"Let's move it," Yuri said, and led the way to the ladder. We climbed up and I sealed the hatch behind us.

I was standing in the room that would be home for the next five days. It was crammed with instruments and storage lockers, except where the windows—ports, to use the right technical term—were. There were fiber optics in the floor so we could check on the legs. The sunlight streaming in lit up the cabin and paled the phosphor panels in the ceiling.

Yuri and I shucked our suits and laid out the maps on the chart table. I took the driver's seat and quickly went through the board check. The lightweight nuclear engine mounted below our deck was fully charged; it would run for years without anything more than an occasional replacement of the circulating fluid elements.

"Why don't you start her off?" Yuri said. "I want to study the maps."

I nodded and slid over to the driver's place. I clicked a few switches and the board in front of me came alive. Red lights winked to green and I revved up the engine. I made the Walker "kneel down" a few times—that is, lowered the bubble—to warm up the hydraulic fluids. It's hard to remember that the legs of the Cat are working at temperatures a hundred degrees below freezing, when you're sitting in a toasty cabin, but it can be dangerous to forget.

While I was doing this I looked out at the life dome rising in the distance. I could pick out people sledding down a hill and farther away a crowd in a snowball fight. A scramble like that is more fun on Ganymede than on Earth; somebody a hundred yards away can pick you off with an accurate shot, because low gravity extends the range of your throwing arm. We don't have anything really spectacular on Ganymede in the way of recreation—nothing like the caverns on Luna, where people can fly around in updrafts, using wings strapped to their backs—but what there is has a lot of zip. For a moment I wished I was out there, in that isolated Earthlike environment, tossing a snowball, instead of piloting a Walker up to the ice fields. I mulled over what Zak had said last night. Then I cut the thought short; it was too late to back out now.

I engaged the engine and the Cat lurched forward. The legs moved methodically, finding the level of the ground and adjusting to it; the gyros kept us upright and shock absorbers cushioned our cabin against the rocking and swaying.

I clicked on the Cat's magnetic screen. The dome area has buried superconductors honeycombing the area, creating a magnetic web. As the Cat left the fringes of the field, we needed more protection from the steady rain of energetic protons. They sleet down on Ganymede from the Van Allen belts. A few hours without protection would fry us. Cat's walls contain superconducting threads carrying high currents. They produce a strong magnetic field outside, which turns incoming charged particles and deflects them.

I took us away from the base at a steady thirty klicks an hour; it would be slower when we hit rough country. The morning sun came slanting in as we moved along the eastern rim of the valley; I switched on the polarizers in our windows to keep down the glare. *Puss* cast a shadow like a marching spider on the slate-gray valley wall.

Maybe I should explain about morning on Ganymede. It's a complicated business. The hardest thing to adjust to when you first land here is the simple fact that Ganymede is a moon, not a planet. It's tied to Jupiter with invisible gravitational apron strings that keep it tide-locked, one face toward Jupiter, always. Meanwhile it revolves around Jove and in turn the Fat One orbits around the sun. The situation is pretty much the same as the Earth-Luna system: Luna shows the same face to Earth and revolves around it in about twenty-eight days, so the lunar "day" —one complete day-night cycle—is twenty-eight days long. Ganymede revolves around Jove in a fraction more than a week, so its "day" is seven Earth days long; the sun is in the sky three and a half days, every week.

This makes a pretty complicated week, believe me. The base has legislated that sunrise occurs at Saturday midnight; it's arbitrary, but it makes for a symmetric week and symmetry is like catnip to scientists. We were starting out Sunday morning and the sun would be in the sky until Wednesday afternoon.

All this time Jove squats square in the middle of the sky, like a striped watermelon. At the moment the sun was streaming through the ports of the Cat and I had to polarize them to cut the glare. Yuri looked up from his map and said, "By the way, that little maneuver back there didn't slip by me."

"What?"

"Don't play dumb. I heard you try to talk Vandez into putting you in charge. It's a good thing he saw through you."

"Well, I don't know," I said slowly. "It seemed to me as long as you didn't know much about a Walker you shouldn't be running one."

"What is there to know? I picked up all I need in a few hours. Here, get out of the seat."

I stopped the Cat and Yuri slid into the driver's chair. We had reached the end of the valley and were heading over a low rise. Here and there ammonia ice clung to the shadows.

Yuri started us forward, staying close to the usual path. The whole trick of guiding a Walker is to keep the legs from having to move very far up and down on each step. It's easier for the machine to inch up a grade than to charge over it.

So the first thing Yuri did was march us directly up the hill. The legs started straining to keep our cabin level and a whining sound filled the air. The Cat teetered, lunged forward, stopped and died.

"Hey!" Yuri said.

"You shouldn't be surprised," I said. "She's just doing what any self-respecting machine does when it's asked to perform the impossible. She's gone on strike. The automatic governor cut in."

Yuri said something incoherent and got up. I took over again and backed us off slowly. Then I nudged the Cat around the base of the hill until I found the signs of a winding path previous Walkers had left. Within fifteen minutes we were in the next valley, its hills lit with the rosy glow of the sun filtering through a thin ammonia cloud overhead.

Chapter 7

We made good time Sunday. I did most of the driving. Yuri gradually picked up the knack of guiding the Cat—I suspected Captain Vandez had him practice only on flat, even ground around the base the day before. The Captain was a spaceman, after all, and groundhog work wasn't his piece of pie.

We slept overnight in the shadow of a thin, tall peak widely used as a landmark; the map called it *Ad Astra*,

Latin for "to the stars." The first time I heard that it sounded a little silly, until I noticed that the peak looks something like a rocket from a distance, if you squint your eyes a little.

Before we turned in for the night I located the way station that was our destination, and camped us next to it. The station wasn't much: just an automatic chemical separator and a set of sampling devices. The chemical plant is vital. It collects water frost that condenses on its outstretched plates—usually a pint a day. The water is automatically stored. Whenever a Walker comes by the driver hooks up his air and water tanks to the station's water reserves and replenishes his supplies.

Where does the station get the air? That's the trick: water is hydrogen and oxygen, so if you could break it up and throw away the hydrogen gas, you would have all the breathable oxygen you need. The Walker does just that—it passes an electric current through water to vaporize it, and then bleeds off the oxygen.

Air isn't just oxygen; the first spacemen found it a lot safer to use a lot of inert nitrogen, too, to keep down the risk of fires. The station extracts nitrogen from the ammonia in the ice all around it, automatically, and has it ready to mix with the oxygen.

Before we bedded down, I connected the air and water hoses from the Walker, clicked a toggle switch on the control board over to FILLING MODE, and forgot about it.

Monday morning the sun was a third of the way across the black sky and Jupiter's banded crescent resembled a Cheshire cat's grin. Yuri fixed a quick-heating breakfast and we set out.

Our route now ran due north. We wove through wrinkled valleys of tumbled stone and pink snowdrifts, keeping an eye open for anything unusual. We were heading for the edge of the "tropical" zone of Ganymede—the belt around the equator where the rock is exposed. Beyond that band lie the blue ice fields. The temperature drops steadily as you leave the equator. If the Walker would take us that far (and if we were crazy) we could have found mountain passes near the north pole nearly two hundred degrees centigrade below freezing.

Slowly, steadily, man is pushing the "tropical" zone toward the poles. Ganymede is warming up.

We avoided the areas near the fusion plants. The big reactors throw out heat and gas at an enormous rate. The ice around them melts and forms churning rivers. The warm water carries heat to neighboring areas and they start melting, too.

There's a limit to the method, though. If you're not careful, your fusion plants will melt their way into Ganymede and get drowned. Ganymede is a big snowball, not a solid world at all. It's mostly water. There's an ice crust about seventy klicks thick, with rock scattered through it like raisins in a pudding. Below that crust Ganymede is slush, a milkshake of water and ammonia and pebbles. There's a solid core, far down inside, with enough uranium in it to keep the slush from freezing.

So the fusion plants don't sit in one place. They're big caterpillars, crawling endlessly outward from the equator. Their computer programs make them seek the surest footing over the outcroppings of rock—only they run on tracks, not feet. We saw one about midday, creeping over a ridgeline in the distance, making about a hundred meters in an hour, sucking in ice and spewing an ammonia-water creek out the tail. It carried a bright orange balloon on top. If it melts its surroundings too fast and gets caught in a lake, it will float until a team can come to fish it out.

Given half a century, they'll give us a thick atmosphere and burn away the toxic gases. Another twenty years and there will be Earth-style air and crops and people on Ganymede. I might live to see that—or maybe by that time I'll be in a Walker on Titan, Saturn's huge moon.

Not that Ganymede was all that cozy now. Our cabin heater ran constantly to fight off the chill that seeped in. Halfway through Monday morning we stopped in a narrow valley and I suited up; the sensor package I had to check out was a klick away, halfway up the side of a hill. The path was too dangerous for the Walker.

I was glad to get the exercise. Ammonia fog boiled up

from the valley and wreathed the peaks ahead. I got so interested in the view I almost missed the package. It was a metal box with scoops and nozzles sticking out in all directions. I opened it up and took out the set of test tube samples I was to carry back. The map had carried a red tag at this one, so I looked it over.

The water collector had a pebble caught in the middle. Probably it lodged there during one of the pint-sized quakes Ganymede has; tidal strains keep the rock and ice sheets butting each other. I replaced a defective bleeder valve in the oxygen sampler and hiked back to the Walker.

After I unsuited I made the mandatory hourly radio call back to the base. A familiar voice answered.

"Zak!" I said. "Don't tell me you're holding up your literary career to stand radio watch."

"Funny man. There isn't anything else to do, with a bum ankle. How are you and Yuri making out?"

"Okay. Say, would you monitor that package I just fixed?"

"Sure, just a minute. Yes, she's sending an all clear now."

We talked for several minutes. There wasn't any important news from the Can and Zak seemed a little bored.

Yuri nudged me. "You guys going to talk forever?"

"Signing off, Zak," I said, and replaced the mike. "What's bugging you, Yuri?"

"Nothing. I just don't think you guys should jam up the airwaves with idle chatter," he said, not looking at me.

It seemed to me he was put out because Zak didn't ask to speak to him. Even Yuri wanted to have some friends; there's nothing like a few days out in the Ganymede wastelands to make you feel lonely.

We stopped several times that day to check out sensor packages. Most of them were at least a few hundred meters from any spot a Walker could reach. They're set up high to keep them out of the gully-washers that sometimes come pouring down the valleys from some distant fusion caterpillar. Yuri and I took turns going out to them; somebody has to stay with the Walker at all times.

I found one package that had been the victim of a quake. The soil under one of its legs had dropped two feet and the package was teetering on the edge of a hole. All its sample tubes had broken.

The third time Yuri went out he came back empty-handed. He couldn't find his package. I violated regs a little—the site was only a city block away from the Walker—and walked out to it with him.

"You know, I remember this spot," I said. "We came by here a few years ago. The package is right around this ledge."

"Well, it's not here now." We were standing by a shelf of yellow rock with boulders scattered around.

"What did the map say was wrong with it?"

Yuri looked around impatiently. "It stopped transmitting a few months ago. That's all they know."

I turned to go. "Well, there's—wait a minute! Isn't that a Faraday cup?"

I bent down and picked up a little bell-like scrap of metal that was lying in the dust. "One of these is usually attached to the top of a sensor package."

I looked at the nearest boulder. It must have weighed a ton, even on Ganymede. "I bet I know where our package is."

We found one other piece of metal wedged under the edge of a boulder. I hiked back and got a replacement package. It took a while to set up and time to put it away from any overhang.

Getting the package's radio zeroed in on the base was a little tricky since we were down in a low trough and had to relay the signals from base through the Walker's radio at first. It took a big chunk out of the day. The next package to be checked was a mile walk from our planned way station for the night. We elected to leave it for morning, but then I got restless and said I would walk out to the site myself.

Jupiter's eclipse of the sun was just ending as I set out. I took a break to watch the sun slip out from behind Jupiter. Suddenly the planet had a rosy halo; we were looking through the outer fringes of the atmosphere. The Can was a distant twinkle of white. I walked along a stream bed and in a way it was like early morning on Earth—as the sun broke out from behind Jupiter things brightened, and the light changed from dull red to a deep yellow. Everything had a clean, sharp look to it. The sun was just a fierce, burning point and there were none of the fuzzy half-shadows you're used to on Earth. Ganymede's man-made atmosphere is still so thin it doesn't blur things.

I felt a *pop*. I stopped dead. I stood still and quickly checked my suit. Nothing on my inboard monitors. My lightpipe scan showed nothing wrong on my back. Suit pressure was normal. I decided it must have been a low-energy micrometeroid striking my helmet; they make a noise but no real damage.

The micrometeroid was probably some uncharged speck of dust, falling into Ganymede's gravity well. If it had been charged, the superconductor threads woven into my suit would have deflected it. Superconductors are a marvel. Once you run a current through them, they keep producing a magnetic field—forever. The field doesn't decay because there's no electrical resistance to the field-producing currents. So even a one-man suit can carry enough magnetic shield to fend off the ferocious Van Allen sleet. And inside the suit there's no magnetic field at all to disturb your instrumentation, if the threads are woven in right. The vector integrals involved in showing that can get messy, especially if you don't know Maxwell's equations from a mud puddle. But the stuff works, and that's all I needed to know.

When I found the sensor package it needed a new circuit module in its radio; the base had guessed the trouble and told me to carry one along on the walk out. That wasn't what interested me, though. This particular package was sitting in the middle of a seeded area. Two years ago a team of biologists planted an acre of microorganisms around it. The organisms were specially tailored in the Lab to live under Ganymede conditions and—we hoped—start producing oxygen, using sunlight and ice and a wisp of atmosphere.

I was a little disappointed when I didn't find a sprawling green swath. Here and there were patches of gray in the soil, so light you couldn't really be sure they were there at all. Over most of the area there was nothing; the organisms had died.

The trouble with being an optimist is that you get to expect too much. The fact that *anything* could live out here was a miracle of bioengineering. I shrugged and turned back the way I had come.

I was almost halfway back to the Cat when I felt an itching in the back of my throat. My eyes flicked down at the dials mounted beneath my transparent viewscreen. The humidity indicator read zero. I frowned.

Every suit has automatic humidity control. You breathe out water vapor and the sublimator subsystem extracts some of it before passing the revived air back to you. The extra water is vented out the back of the suit. You'd think that if the microprocessor running the subsystem failed, you'd get high humidity.

But I had too little. In fact, none.

I flipped down my rear lightpipe and squinted at my backpack. Water dripped from the lower vent. I checked my—

Dripped? I looked at it again.

That shouldn't happen. The suit should have been venting water slowly, so it vaporized instantly when it reached the extremely thin atmosphere outside. Dripping meant the relief valve was open and all my water had been purged.

I called up a systems review on my side viewplate, just below eye level inside my helmet. From the data train I guessed the humidity control crapout had been running for over half an hour. *That* was what had made the popping noise. And I had written it off as a micrometeroid. Wishful thinking.

I stepped up my pace. The tickle at the back of my throat meant I might have suit throat. That's the overall name for anything related to breathing processed air. If you get contaminants in the mix, or just lose water vapor, your throat and nose soon dry out, or get irritated. A dry throat is a feasting ground for any bacteria hanging around. If you're lucky, the outcome is just a sore throat that hangs around for a while.

I hustled. Off in the distance I could see the faint aura of orange from a fusion caterpillar. The rising mist from its roaring fusion exhaust diffused the light for tens of klicks. Blue-green shadows in the eroded hillsides contrasted with the gentle orange glow. Suddenly Ganymede felt strange and more than a little threatening.

I was glad when the Cat came within sight. It was backed up to the way station. I clumped up the ladder and wedged through the narrow lock into the cabin.

"You're in time for the feast," Yuri said.

"Hope I can taste it."

"Why?"

I opened my mouth and pointed. Yuri looked in, turned my head toward the light, looked again. "It is a little red. You should look after it."

I got out the first-aid kit and found the anesthetic throat spray. It tasted metallic but it did the job; after a moment it didn't hurt to swallow.

I broke down the humidity control unit in my suit. Sure enough, the microprocessor had a fault. I took a replacement chip slab out of storage and made the change. Everything worked fine.

I was surprised at how much Yuri could do with our rations. We had thin slices of chicken in a thick mushroom sauce, lima beans that still had some snap in them, and fried rice. We topped it off with strawberry cream cake and a mug of hot tea. Pretty damned elegant, considering.

"My compliments," I said. "That was undoubtedly the best meal within a million miles." I felt giddy.

"Some compliment," Yuri said. "That means I'm better than the base cafeteria."

I got up from the pullout shelf that we used for a table. The room began to revolve. I put out my hand to steady myself.

"Say!" Yuri shouted. He jumped up and grabbed my arm. The room settled down again.

"I—I'm okay. A little dizzy."

"You're pale."

"The light is poor in ultraviolet here. I'm losing my suntan," I said woozily.

"It must be more than that."

"You're right. Think I'll go to bed early."

"Take some medicine. I think you have suit throat."

I grinned weakly. "Maybe it's something I ate." I

jerked on the pull ring and my foldout bunk came down.
Yuri brought the first-aid kit over. I sat on the bunk taking
off my clothes and wondered vaguely where second aid
would come from if the first aid failed. I shook my head;
the thinking factory had shut down for the night. Yuri
handed me a pill and I swallowed it. Then a tablet, which
I sucked on. Finally I got between the covers and found
myself studying some numbers and instructions that were
stenciled on the ceiling of the cabin. Before I could figure
out what they meant I fell asleep.

The morning was better, much better. Yuri woke me
and gave me a bowl of warm broth. He sat in a deck chair
and watched me eat it.

"I must call the base soon," he said.

"Um."

"I have been thinking about what to say."

"Um . . . Oh. You mean about me?"

"Yes."

"Listen, if Captain Vandez thinks I'm really sick he'll
scrub the rest of the trip. We'll have to go back."

"So I thought."

"Do me a favor, will you? Don't mention this when
you call in. I'm feeling better. I'll be okay."

"Well—"

"Please?"

"All right. I don't want this journey ruined just because you are careless." He slapped his knees and got up.
"I will make the call."

"Mighty nice of you," I mumbled. I dozed for a
while. I was feeling better, but I was a little weak. I heard
Yuri talking to Zak briefly. I ran over the route we would
follow that day. The next way station was a respectable
distance away and there was only one sensor package to
visit. We would have to spend our time making tracks for
the next station—which was just as well, with one crew
member on the woozy side.

"Yuri," I said, "check and be sure we got our tanks
filled with air and water. It's a long way to the next—"

"Bohles, you may be sick but that doesn't mean you
can start ordering me around. I will get us there."

I rolled over and tried to go to sleep. I heard Yuri suit up and go out. A little later there were two faint *thunks* as the hoses disconnected from the way station. Then Yuri came back in, unsuited and sat down in the driver's chair.

The Cat lurched forward and then settled down to a steady pace. I decided to stop worrying and let Yuri handle things for a while. I was feeling better every minute, but another forty winks wouldn't do any harm. I let the gentle swaying of the Walker rock me to sleep.

I woke around noon; I must have been more tired than I thought. Yuri tossed me a self-heating can of corned beef; I opened it and devoured the contents immediately.

I passed the next hour or so reading a novel. Or rather, I tried. I dozed off and woke up in mid-afternoon. There was a lot of sedative in that medicine.

I got up, pulled on my coveralls and walked over to the control board. "Walked" isn't quite the right word—with my bunk and the table down, the Cat resembled a roomy telephone booth.

I sat down next to Yuri. We were making good time across a flat, black plain. There was an inch or so of topsoil—dust, really—that puffed up around the Cat's feet as they stepped. The dust comes from the cycle of freezing and thawing of ammonia ice caught in the boulders. The process gradually fractures the Ganymede rock, breaking it down from pebbles to shards to BB shot to dust. In a century or so somebody will grow wheat in the stuff.

Some of the soil is really specks of interplanetary debris that has fallen on Ganymede for the last three billion years. All over the plain were little pits and gouges. The bigger meteors had left ray craters, splashing white across the reddish-black crust. The dark ice is the oldest stuff on Ganymede. A big meteor can crack through it, throwing out bright, fresh ice. The whole history of the solar system is scratched out on Ganymede's ancient scowling face, but we still don't know quite how to read all the scribblings. After the fusion bugs have finished, a lot of the intricate, grooved terrain will be gone. A little sad, maybe—the terraced ridges are beautiful in the slanting yellow rays of sunset—but there are others like them, on other moons. The solar system has a whole lot more snowball moons like Ganymede than it has habitable spots for people. Just like every other age in human history, there are some sad choices to make.

Yuri sidestepped a thick-lipped crater, making the servos negotiate the slope without losing speed. He had caught the knack pretty fast. The bigger craters had glassy rims, where the heat of impact had melted away the roughness. Yuri could pick his way through that stuff with ease. I leaned back and admired the view. Io's shadow was a tiny dot on Jupiter's eternal dancing bands. The thin little ring made a faint line in the sky, too near Jupiter to really see clearly. You had to look away from it, so your side vision could pick it out. There was a small moon there, I knew, slowly breaking up under tidal stresses and feeding stuff into the ring. It's too small to see from Ganymede, though. You get the feeling, watching all these dots of light swinging through the sky, that Jupiter's system is a giant clockwork, each wheel and cog moving according to intricate laws. Our job was to fit into this huge cosmic machine, without getting mashed in the gears.

I yawned, letting all these musing drop away, and glanced at the control board. "You do a full readout this morning?"

Yuri shrugged. "Everything was in order last night."

"Huh. Here—" I punched in for a systems inventory. Numbers and graphs rolled by on the liquid display. Then something went red.

"Hey. Hey. B and C tanks aren't filled," I said tensely.

"What? I put the system into filling mode last night. The meter read all right this morning."

"Because you've got it set on A tank. You have to fill each independently, and check them. For Chrissakes—!"

"Why is that? Was that your idea? It's stupid to not combine the entire system. I—"

"Look," I said rapidly, "the Cat sometimes carries other gasses, for mining or farming. If the computer control automatically switched from A to B to C, you could end up breathing carbon dioxide, or whatever else you were carrying."

"Oh."

"I showed you that a couple days back."

"I suppose I forgot. Still—"

"Quiet," I did a quick calculation. With only a third of our oxy capacity filled—correction, we'd used some already—and on our present course—

"We won't make it to our next station," I announced.

Yuri kept his eyes on his driving. He scowled. "What about our suits?" he asked slowly. "They might have some air left."

"Did you recharge yours when you came back in?"

"Ah . . . no."

"I didn't either." Another screw-up.

I checked them anyway. Not much help, but some. I juggled figures around on the clipboard, but you can't sidestep simple arithmetic. We were in deep trouble.

Yuri stepped up the Cat's pace. It clanked and bounced over slabs of jutting purple ice. "I conclude," he said, "that we should call the base and ask for assistance."

I frowned. "I don't like to do it."

"Why? We must."

"Somebody will have to fly out here and drop air packs. There's always some risk, because even Ganymede's thin air has winds in it. We don't understand those winds yet."

"I see." Yuri gave me a guarded look. "An extra mission. It would not sit well with Commander Aarons, would it?"

"Probably not." I could tell Yuri was thinking that when the report came to be written, he'd get the blame. "But look, the real point is that somebody back at base would have to risk his neck, and all because of a dumb mistake."

Yuri was silent. The Walker rocked on over the broken ground. A thin pink ammonia stream flowed in the distance.

"You may not like it," he said, "but I do not intend to die out here." He reached for the radio, turned it on, and picked up the microphone.

"Wait," I said. "I may . . ."

"Yah?"

"Let's see that map." I studied it for several minutes.

I pointed out a spot to Yuri and said, "There, see the gully that runs off this valley?"

"Yes. So what?"

I drew a straight line from the gully through the hills to the next broad plain. The line ran through a red dot on the other side of the hills. "That's a way station, that dot. I've been there before. We're slated to check it in two days, on our way back. But I can reach it by foot from that gully, by hiking over the hills. It's only seven kilometers."

"You couldn't make it."

I worried over the map some more. A few minutes later I said, "I *can* do it. There's a series of streambeds I can follow most of the distance; that'll cut out a lot of climbing." I worked the calculator. "Even allowing for the extra exertion, our oxy will last."

Yuri shrugged. "Okay, boy scout. Just so you leave me enough to cover the time you're gone, plus some extra so a rocket from the base can reach me if you crap out."

"Why don't you walk yourself?"

"I'm in favor of calling the base right now. But I'll wait out your scheme if you want, right here, without budging an inch. I don't like risks."

"There's a chance that rocket plane might foul up and crash, too. At least my way we can do something to help ourselves and not sit around on our hands waiting for assistance."

"Those are my terms, Bohles. If you go, you go alone."

I grimaced. It was a lousy, stinking mess with no good solutions. "Look, Yuri . . ." I began.

"Stuff it, Bohles. I will not try a crazy scheme for the sake of your pride."

"*Pride*?" I said between clenched teeth.

Yuri leaned back casually in the pilot's chair. "You have absolutely got to be in first place. You're Matt Bohles, mama's little boy. Always have to win. Hell, look what you do on vacation—run around doing the dog work for the base."

"I do it because I like it."

"Then you're dumber than you look, goody-boy."

"You stupid son of a bitch—"

"No melodramatics, kid." He looked at me carefully, calculating, but I was too angry to think what that meant. "Come on, we're wasting oxygen. What is going to win: common sense or pride?"

"You frapping bastard—"

"Eh, goody-goody?"

I was boiling. I should've smacked him, but when I raised my hand something inside me cringed. I saw that dazzling noon sunshine, the dry schoolyard, that gang beating me—

I stopped. *I've got to get away*, I thought. I didn't stop to think that Yuri was herding me just the way he wanted to.

I turned and yanked my suit off the cabin wall. I didn't think, I acted.

The cold seeped into my legs. Pink slabs of ice, gray rock, black sky—and always the thin rasp of my breath, throat raw from coughing. My helmet air was thick and foul. I stumbled along sluggishly.

Pride. The anger boiled up in me again and I quickened my pace. *Pride*. I'd fix that bastard. I'd show him I was braver than he was, and smarter, not afraid of anything. I'd—

The gravel slipped under my boot and I nearly lost my balance. A small landslide eroded away the footing I had. I couldn't stop to rest—I had to keep moving up the slope, even though my breath was ragged and I was sweating.

Seven klicks, yeah. A short hop. I felt like it had been seven years since I left the Cat, and still I hadn't started down the incline onto the plain.

I struggled up the side of what seemed to be a sand dune, my breath tearing at my throat. The streambed shown on my map had vanished and I was pushing on over broken, hilly terrain. Every fifteen minutes I checked in with Yuri, but I was damned if I was going to ask him for help. Pride goeth before a fall, ha ha. And my throat hurt, my nose dribbled, my eyes stung. Everything tasted oily— air, rations, water.

The stones and sand gritted against my boots, slipping away, robbing me of balance and speed. I toiled up the incline, angling across. A few boulders buried in the silt helped. I could pull myself up with them for support. The gray line that was the top drew gradually nearer as I lurched along, cursing my own stupidity. It promised nothing—a few random rocks were perched there, sheltering patches of snow.

Then I reached it.

And looked beyond, down the face of the hill. The blue way station beckoned serenely in the distance. It was two kilometers away down a broad swarth of bare rock. I could reach it in half an hour.

I'd won.

Won what? I thought. For who? *Why did I do this?*

Chapter 8

So I got extra oxy from the way station, rested, ate, and hiked back. It was an anticlimactic return—Yuri hardly said anything. I told myself he felt embarrassed.

I didn't feel particularly comfortable with him, to say the least. I did a lot of hiking out to visit sensor packages, glad to be on my own.

By sundown Wednesday we were heading south and angling back toward the base. There's no true night on Ganymede because Jove hangs there, beaming down a hundred times brighter than Earth's full moon. After all, it fills 250 times as much of the sky as Luna does from Earth. So night is really a sort of yellowish twilight; the jagged valleys turn beautiful and spooky all at once. All they need is a moaning wind and an abandoned castle or two, to complete the eerie picture.

We shambled into the base late Thursday night, a little behind schedule and tired. Zak was standing outside waiting for us, along with the mechanic who would check out the Cat to be sure we hadn't hot rodded her to death.

Mechanics are like mother hens, clucking over their machines. This one poked around for half an hour before he gave us an okay. Neither Yuri nor I mentioned the problem with the air tanks; someone would wonder why we hadn't reported it earlier. I had already had enough red tape for one day.

I told Zak about it, though, over supper.

"It saddens me, Matt boy, to see you picking up bad habits. The rule book plainly says that such little dramas should be reported." He gave me an appraising look. "On the other hand, creative rule-bending is an art form we must all learn, sooner or later."

"Looking back on it," I said, "I'm not so sure I did the right thing."

"Look upon it as a valuable learning experience," Zak said grandly.

"My conscience bothers me."

"Oh? What's it feel like? I had mine taken out, along with my appendix."

"I suspected as much."

"I think I can lay your pangs to rest, Matt. Yuri reported the whole thing, after the fact."

"Huh?"

"I was on radio watch, remember? Let me consult the Encyclopedia of All Knowledge—" he picked up the binder lying on the bench next to him—"and all will be clear."

"What's that?"

"My diary. You can't read upside-down writing, I take it? Good, my secrets are safe." He opened the binder and ran a finger along to the right entry. "Ah, yes. You called me, said nothing worth immortalizing with a note. Um. Then Yuri called—said you were outside, visiting a sensor package—and asked to speak to Captain Vandez. On a private line." He raised an eyebrow. "Interesting."

"So Yuri reported it anyway. I didn't think he had it in him."

"Nor I. Maybe he's not such a rat after all."

"Um. No comment."

"Cynic."

"Um."

*　　*　　*

I managed to get in a morning's skiing before the *Sagan* lifted off. It was fun to feel a chill wind whipping by my ears, lean into a turn and slash a trail across a hillside. Everybody was out in the dome for a last bit of exercise and we all got into an immense snowball fight an hour before liftoff. After I caught two in a row down the back of my collar I surrendered and went back to pack.

Liftoff was uneventful. By the time Captain Vandez let us out of our seats Ganymede was shrinking rapidly and neither Zak nor I could make out much surface detail. Far away we could see some of the other moons. Io is an orange pizza, volcano-pocked. Europa has a planet-sized glacier and crinkly ridges as tangled as spaghetti. Callistro is a shotgun pattern of overlapping craters. There are thirty-nine Jovian moons in all bigger than ten kilometers across, and lots smaller than that. By the time early expeditions reached J-8 they were tired of the whole business and nobody has even landed on the last four relatively large ones. No reason to—anybody who cares can see them close up if he can get time on the Lab's big telescope, the Far Eye.

I woke up just before the *Sagan* docked at the Lab. Zak had fallen asleep in the middle of composing a poem and gave every appearance of being no longer in the land of the living. He had sprawled out over two seats and was teetering on the edge, about to fall into the aisle. I elbowed him awake and we queued up at the air lock.

The *Sagan* was moored above the top of the Can. When I came out of the lock I was looking down the bore of an enormous gun—or at least, that's the way it seemed. I was faced down, looking through the hollow center section of the Can—the ship bay. I could see red and white stars out the other end, and the dark outlines of shuttles and skimmers floating around the axial cylinder, being serviced.

I hooked on to a throw line and scooted across to the personnel lock, the same one we'd come out nine days before. The week on Ganymede had given me a touch of groundhog legs—a sense that there really ought to be an up and down, so that I kept looking around for a reference. Going through the personnel lock fouled me up even further, because for a moment I was convinced that I was falling down it. Don't ask me to explain why; it's just a reflex, like sneezing. Zak felt it, too; he started spinning his arms for balance the second he came through the lock, which just made him tumble until he stopped it.

We followed the line through a series of tubes and ended up in a big room so long the curvature hid the heads of people standing against the far wall.

"Ah, gentlemen. 'And the hunter, home from the hill.' Welcome back."

I turned and found Ishi smiling at me.

"The first thing he does is quote a rival poet to me," Zak said, and pumped Ishi's hand when I was finished with it.

"You look thinner," I said. "Working too hard?"

"What's new?" Zak said.

"Not much. We lost another bathyscaphe-type probe in Jupiter's atmosphere, but it found nothing new before it failed. And no, Matt, there has been little work for me. I do have to go out tonight to correct a drifting setting in a satellite, however."

"Tonight? But that's the amateur hour," I said.

"Correct. I understand you will play guitar. I regret missing it."

"Don't," Zak said. "I've heard him practice."

"Oh, a music critic, too?"

"Come along, Ishi, such louts don't recognize a renaissance man when they see one."

"Wait, we have to get our luggage."

The panel behind me slid aside and two men struggled in with a net of baggage. They unslipped a knot and the cases tumbled slowly out; in a one-tenth-g field nothing could be damaged. I located our bags near the top of the stack and started to reach for them.

"You boys are standing directly in front of my suitcases," a familiar voice said.

"These are ours, lady," Zak said.

"Don't you think I know my *own*—Captain! Captain Vandez!"

"The Captain is not here, ma'am," a man said.

"I demand—"

"Here's your case, Zak," I said. "Ishi—catch!" I threw him one of mine and snatched up Zak's other bag.

"Don't let them get away. They have one of my—"

I showed the man the names stenciled on the cases. He nodded.

"I know your names, boys! Don't think you can—"

We circled around the pile and I scooped up my second case. The man was talking to her as we went out the door.

"Good grief," Zak said, "who *is* that woman?"

"Mrs. Schloffski," Ishi said. "It is rumored that her husband was appointed to the Laboratory through political influence."

"The ISA has a lot to answer for," I said.

"Matt!" My father had just come out of a side corridor. Jenny was with him. We all shook hands and I kissed Jenny. She held the kiss a little longer than I expected. It was top quality goods.

"I've got to go pamper a shuttle right now," Jenny said, an arm around me, "but when I come off my shift. . ."

"Fine," I said. "I'll even give you preference over my guitar. I still have some practicing to do before tonight."

"Well," Jenny said, wrinkling her nose. "I suppose I will have to take what I can get." She gave me a peck on the cheek and walked away.

"What next?" Zak said. "Now that Matt here has beaten off the hordes of panting women that follow him everywhere, what say we snag a milkshake and discuss the adventures of our brave heroes amid the terrible snows of Ganymede?"

"I'm afraid not," Dad said. "Matt has to go home."

"Oh," Ishi and Zak said together.

"Well, next time," Zak finished lamely.

"See you tonight," I said. "Ishi, put our names in for time in the squash court. I'm going to beat you yet."

Ishi smiled and waved good-bye. Dad and I made our way home through the tubes, talking about minor events that had happened in Monitoring while I was away. They were registering more and more of the unusual debris from outside Jupiter's moon system. The chunks of rock usually spiraled in and entered Jupiter's atmosphere near the poles.

"Could it be a meteor shower from the asteroid belt?" I said.

"That is one theory," Dad said. He seemed distracted and didn't add anything more.

Mom wasn't there when we got home; Dad said she was in Hydroponics, working late. I unpacked, crammed my gear into the cubbyholes the Lab calls closets, and came back out to the living room. Dad was sitting at the dining table; his hands were clasped together.

"Sit down."

I did.

"I talked to Commander Aarons about you yesterday. Captain Vandez mentioned you in his weekly report from Ganymede."

"Oh?"

"Yes. I must admit it surprised me. I did not think you would make such an error."

"Huh?"

"I'm talking about the trouble you and Yuri had."

"What trouble?"

Dad grimaced. "The air hose. Captain Vandez reported that you failed to attach it properly, did not notice the mistake, and almost killed both yourself and Yuri. And that you would not report the incident yourself—Yuri had to do it."

"What!"

"It was a good thing Yuri managed to get to that way station. I realize the basic idea was yours, and Yuri reported that, which was a good thing. It made you look better in Captain Vandez's eyes, so that he did not reprimand you in person. If Yuri had not gotten to that station in time, the Captain would have had to send a ship out to save you. Then it would have gone very badly for you. As things stand—"

"Dad!"

"What?"

"That's a bunch of lies!"

"I am simply repeating what Commander—"

"I know, but it's all wrong. *I* didn't foul up the air hose. Yuri did it."

"That isn't the way it was reported."

"But that's the way it *was*. That goon didn't—"

"Hummm. Wait a moment. Can you prove any of this?"

"Prove—? Well, no, I—"

"Yuri radioed in the report, You—according to Captain Vandez—never mentioned the subject afterward, when you were on the air. He thought you were simply too embarrassed to own up. Captain Vandez said he thought Yuri had been quite fair to you, considering, and he did not regard the matter as too serious."

"Well, *I* do," I said sharply. "Yuri turned in a false report."

"What really happened?"

I told him. He wondered whether Zak could give any testimony that would back me up. I decided not; I had never said anything over the air that would prove my version of events.

"I hate to say this," Dad said, "but it appears Yuri has the edge on you. He reported the incident. You did not. Silence on your part is hard to explain."

"I know. That's what I get for cutting corners on the regulations."

"You should have reported in sick in the first place."

"And I should have blown the whistle on Yuri when he gummed things up. I thought the job was more important than a bunch of rules."

"The rules are there to insure your safety. All of us are living in a hostile environment. It pays to be careful."

"I know, I know." I sighed and leaned on the dining table, my face in my hands.

"Son, don't take it too hard. I do not believe Commander Aarons considers it to be of overriding importance. It will not weigh too heavily when the decision is made about your staying on at the Lab. I'll speak to him about the incident, anyway, and give your side of the story. That should count for something."

"Thanks, Dad." I looked around. "That's why Mom's not here, isn't it? So you could talk to me."

He nodded. "And to give you some quiet for your guitar practice. The show is only a couple of hours from now."

"Right." I made a weak smile and got up. I went into my room and sat on the foldout bed, resting my guitar on my legs. I practiced series of chords, to limber up my fingers, and then ran through the pieces I planned to play.

Inside, I was still reeling from what Dad had told me. Sure, I was never a bosom buddy of Yuri's, but this—!

After a while I put the thoughts aside. It didn't do any good to brood, and there was no point in being depressed during the amateur hour. I could rail against my fate after I was through playing. So I threw my shoulders back, shook my head to clear it, and played carefully through each piece, looking for errors or places where I allowed my fingers to slur over a passage, losing precision and blurring a chord here and there. If a classical guitarist plays a piece often enough without sharp concentration, he gets sloppy. The guitarist can become blind to his own work; the audience doesn't, though. Segovia I'm not, but anything I played was going to be the best I could do.

Dad stuck his head in. "Supper?"

I shook my head. Then something nibbling away in the back of my mind made me say, "Dad? Remember the talk we had before I went to Ganymede?"

"Yes."

"You said—or implied—the head of BioTech Division had advance information about the Lab maybe shipping us kids back. BioTech—that's Yuri's father, isn't it?"

"Yes, that's a Sagdaeff. He has good political connections Earthside. I don't understand politicians—never learned to smile without meaning it—but I think Sagdaeff wants to parley the rearrangement, if it happens, into a promotion for himself. Maybe he's fishing for Aaron's job."

"Interesting," I said thoughtfully. "Do you think there's really going to be a scaledown, Dad?"

"I gave up reading tea leaves long ago," he said. "I shouldn't have told you this gossip, either. Back to the guitar, son." He gave me a slap on the back. I realized he was probably trying to distract me from thinking about Yuri. So I started plucking and strumming again, and pretty soon I was immersed in the music.

Dad came back an hour later, whistling, to remind me that it was time to dress. I put on the only formal clothes I have: a black suit with broad lapels, cut back severely in the style of five years ago. Mom had let out the seams as much as possible but the inevitable had caught up with me; the pants pinched, my stockings showed stretches, and she'd had to piece the shoulders so I wouldn't lose blood circulation in my arms. It didn't matter much that the suit was hopelessly out of fashion on Earth— everybody else in the Lab was in the same boat, and anyway I liked the sequins on the cutaway lapels on the jacket.

Dad and I walked to the central auditorium, me lugging my guitar case. People were already filling the bowl of seats. Jenny was waiting outside. She squeezed my hand and wished me good luck and I made small talk. I didn't want to tell anybody about the Ganymede trouble and at the same time I couldn't think of anything else, so I must have sounded like a dodo. After a few minutes of monosyllables from me Jenny gave up and went to find a seat.

Backstage was a hubbub with people carrying props and sets around, women touching up their makeup and a few trying to learn their lines at the last minute. I found a corner to wait in and sat down.

I could hear Commander Aarons introducing the program; his deep voice boomed out over the crowd without need of a microphone. Almost everyone in the Can was there. The auditorium is pretty far inward toward the axis, so gravity there is only a small fraction of a g.

The first act used that fact to advantage: it was a family team I'd watched before, performing ballet feats that would be impossible on Earth. They leaped and whirled and threw each other high in the air. It made you feel light and carefree yourself, just looking at them.

Mr. and Mrs. Bhadranin went on next. She plays tabula while her husband performs on the sitar, an Indian instrument. It was beautiful. Mr. Bhadranin let me fool around with his sitar once and I came away impressed; compared to it the guitar is a kazoo. Mastering the sitar is impossible—men simply devote their lives to it and try to achieve as much as possible. It's not an instrument for a dabbler like me.

A bunch from Maintenance followed. They did an involved skit about how messy the other divisions of the Lab were. The skit ended with everybody being forced to live outside the Can because the interior was crammed with garbage. I suppose it was funny, because people laughed a lot. I wasn't paying attention; I was going on next.

The skit ended. I picked up my guitar—I'd tuned it during the bursts of laughter—and stopped at the edge of the curtain for Commander Aarons to introduce me.

The Commander is a big, stocky man with a grizzled moustache and a lot of smile lines around his mouth. He keeps up his ruddy tan and always looks like he's in perfect health. That's why I noticed the difference this time. He was standing off to the side of the stage, talking to one of the Lab officers. The Commander was scowling. His face had turned pale. He asked the officer a question, listened, and then looked across the stage at me.

He made a gesture for me to stay put. The Commander walked to the center of the stage and held up a hand. The crowd quieted.

"I am afraid the rest of tonight's program will not be presented," he said. There was a questioning hum from the audience.

"Tonight, while on duty and conducting satellite maintenance, Ishi Moto was killed by a small meteoroid. His death was instantaneous. The chunk of rock that struck him was only the size of a dime, but it was moving very fast.

"Ishi was a fine boy. I do not think it appropriate that we continue this program. Good evening."

Chapter 9

There isn't much to say about the rest of that night. At first I could not believe it: as soon as the curtain was drawn I rushed over to Commander Aarons and asked, disbelieving, if I had heard him correctly. Hadn't it been someone else, somebody with a name that sounded like Ishi?

Even as I said it I knew I was trying to run away from the truth, cover it up, pretend it wasn't there. I turned away from the Commander and automatically, mechanically put my guitar back in its case. The air seemed heavy and warm.

I remember making my way out of the auditorium. I met my parents. I talked to Jenny. She was crying and I suddenly found that I was, too. Jenny and I stood in the middle of the crowd, crying and sobbing and holding each other, almost without knowing what we were doing. It was incredible. Ishi, gone. Forever.

After a few moments I recovered a bit. Zak was there; I hadn't seen him before. He took Jenny away and I left with my parents. Suddenly I wanted to get away from that place and away from people.

We said nothing during the walk home. The terrible thing was there was nothing to do. I guess there never is. Our society has no required ritual for friends and relatives of someone who has died. Instead, they sit and stare at each other and feel awkward, useless. They have no way to take the edge off their grief. I thought about that for a while until I realized that I was using the idea as a way to avoid thinking about Ishi, because that was too painful. And, of course, that thought made me feel even more rotten.

When we got home I went to my room. There didn't seem to be anything to say to my parents, or to anybody.

Ishi's job had been one of the dangerous ones, sure, but the computed chances of a man ever being hit were infinitesimal. His death was a fantastic piece of bad luck. Space suits provide some protection against low-velocity meteoroids, but there isn't much that can be done about a pebble traveling faster than a rifle bullet.

The Lab does what it can. We've search out the dust clouds and small swarms of gravel orbiting Jupiter. When a shuttle goes out, the trajectory is programmed to keep the craft moving in the same direction as the matter around it, so that most of the tiny debris isn't zipping by the shuttle. The best insurance is a fast trip, so the pilot spends as little time possible outside the Can.

All these things are fine, but they can't add up to absolute safety. We don't know enough about the junk circling Jupiter and we never will—radar won't pick up small chips of rock.

So I laid in bed and thought about these things. And remembered Ishi. And wondered how many times in my life I would say good-bye to a friend, suspecting nothing, and then never see him again. It took me a long time to get to sleep.

The next morning our family went to extend condolences to Ishi's family. We sat on the floor and conversed, almost whispering. Most of our talk was of inconsequential things: flower arranging, the comings and goings of people we both knew, the subtlety of watercolor prints. We spoke only briefly of Ishi.

We attended the service for Ishi together. His body was returned to the life cycle of the Can by breaking it down and distributing the elements to the chemical vats. Preserving the body and things of that sort are barbaric.

We followed the Moto family to their home and spoke for a long while. We were served green tea. We smiled, nodded. We went home.

I found the experience strangely satisfying. The Moto family maintained its serenity; it even buoyed up the friends who came to call. I promised myself that I would not let the Moto family slip out of contact; I could learn much from them.

* * *

I moped around the apartment for half an hour and then went to class. I was having trouble with calculus and needed a session with the teaching machines. Our machines are better than the run-of-the-mill ones used in classrooms Earthside—they're linked to the Lab computer, which can do two dozen different jobs at once and still fool you into thinking it's as smart as a human being, even though the computer is only using a fraction of its capacity.

If you can justify the expense, you can get a big slice of the computer's capability assigned to you. Then "David" —that's what the computer techs call it (or rather him) —sounds like a genius. You can discuss quantum mechanics, economic theory, stellar exploration, or theology with David and he will give solid, well-researched answers as fast as you can read them. (I tried theology; he said God was one of man's better ideas.) He's a gift from heaven when you're doing a term paper. On the other hand, David has a weak personality and never makes a joke. Machines do have their limitations. But one of these days some engineer will give David a sense of humor and overnight he'll become a television personality. Until then, though, I find him a bit dull.

I spent two hours with David, wading knee-deep through calculus exercises. David pounds away at a point until you feel as though you've been sandbagged. Then, just when you're sure you are a mental defective, you understand—usually because David has finally found the way to present an idea so that it fits your particular bias.

David isn't just a storage bank for a lot of information. He is a psychologist, a judge, and a coach; just like a human teacher, only many times faster.

This time he gave me a real workout. I left the booth feeling groggy. Zak was outside, looking the other way down a corridor.

"Directing traffic?" I said.

"No, just wondering why Yuri beat it."

"He was out here?"

"Until a second ago, yes. I was going to ask him something and he ducked away."

"That was just when I came out?"

"I guess so. What's up?"

"Let's go have some coffee. I'll bring you up to date."

After I had told him Zak whistled and rocked back in his chair. "A clever boy, that Yuri. No mouth breather, he. Who would have suspected he was such a snake?"

"You. Me."

"We were prejudiced from the start. The question of the hour is, now that you are in the soup, how do we get you out?"

"My father will talk to the Commander."

"And our good Commander, with contradicting testimony and all the evidence on one side—"

"Will believe Yuri's story."

"True. The man has his limitations."

"I'm going to forget the whole thing." I shrugged. "Yuri has me boxed in."

"The Bohles I know doesn't give up."

"The Bohles you know is no fool, either. Commander Aarons can't do anything, officially, without evidence. His hands are tied. There's no use in my whining to him about it."

"A point, a definite point."

Then I told Zak what Dad had said about Yuri's father. I expected him to react immediately; instead, he sat and pondered, eyes narrowed, for a long moment.

"You realize the implications, of course?" he said.

"Such as—?"

"Yuri's father heard a cutback is coming. He guessed —or learned—that only one or two of us kids would stay. Then he told Yuri—"

"—who put two and two together—"

"—and got the square root of sixteen, after double-checking it with the computer. He figured you were prime competition, Matt. So he set out to be conspicuous—good at chess, a winner in squash, a hard worker for Atmospheric Studies, helping with the Walker on Ganymede."

"And he got me so frapping mad I took a risk on Ganymede. Then he took credit for it, and threw mud all over me in Commander Aarons' eyes. *Damn!*"

"Neat. Very, very neat. The hell of it is, you've got no comeback."

"I suppose not." I sighed. "I'd rather not think about it anyway, not right now. This little scramble is pretty small stuff compared to Ishi."

Zak's face clouded over. "Yeah." He hunched over the rec room table. Neither of us said anything. Zak spilled some of his coffee and instead of sponging it up he stared down at it, distracted. He poked a finger into the brown stain and began tracing a watery design in the smooth, shiny surface. I felt like hell.

"Look, I think I'll go put in some time in Monitoring," I said, getting up. "My watch comes up in an hour and I might as well try being early once, just as an experiment. Take—"

"Matt Bohles?" A secretary from down the hall stuck his head in the door.

"Yes?"

"There is a call for you. You can take it on the student recreation center telephone."

"Oh, okay." I hoisted aboard my notes, waved to Zak and jogged down the hall. The corridor curved up, giving the familiar illusion that I was running uphill. In a sense I was, because trotting in this direction I was moving counter to the Can's rotation, which is harder than going the opposite way. For short distances the effect is unnoticeable; only when you're going nearly halfway around the rim of the Can does it pay to stop and think about the fastest way to travel. But today I had other things to think about.

I found the rec center phone and picked it up.

"Matt?" my father's voice said.

"What's up? I was headed toward Monitoring—"

"Never mind that. I have been speaking to Commander Aarons. He wishes to talk to you. In his office."

When I got there Jenny was seated quietly on a couch. That surprised me more than anything else; what could she be doing here?

Dad was sitting in a chair, holding a sheaf of papers. The Commander looked up when I came in, said hello and motioned me to a popout seat.

"Your father brought to my attention a somewhat

different version of the events on Ganymede," Commander Aarons said, leaning forward and resting his folded hands on his desk top. "I do not mind saying that I am in something of a quandary. I must take a judicial position, since there exists conflicting testimony. At the same time there is no way to determine the truth; there were no other witnesses."

He stopped and grimaced. The movement tilted his moustache at an angle and gave him a red nose. "Therefore, young Mister Bohles, I shall drop the matter. No action will be taken. Both your and Yuri Sagdaeff's stories are now known to me; I may or may not consider them in future evaluations of your performance."

The Commander stopped and let out a breath. "And that is that." He reached out and flipped off a switch set into the top of his desk. "That's the official recording for ship's log. As far as regulations go the matter is now dead." He looked at me and smiled. "But that is not the reason I had your father call you."

"Sir?"

"I was wondering if you would be interested in changing jobs. You would work with Miss Fleming here."

"Huh? Outside?"

"Operating a shuttle," my father said, "and making satellite repairs. The job Ishi had."

Now I understood why Jenny was here. "Who recommended me?"

The Commander tapped a fingernail on the display screen mounted flat into his desk top. I could see some typed entries in what looked like a personnel form. "Your record," he said. "You know electronics. You have maneuvered one-man shuttlecraft into parking stations."

"And you have good no-g reflexes," Dad said.

"I see." I still didn't like the idea of getting a job because Jenny put my name in. "But why so soon? Ishi's job wasn't all that urgent. Why do you need a replacement right away?"

"The storms," Jenny said.

I looked over at her. It was the first sound she had made since I came in the room.

"Correct," my father said. "They are coming more

often now and they are more intense. The entire upper atmosphere of Jupiter, particularly near the poles, seems to be in turmoil. The satellites keep track of this; if they fail we're left with nothing."

"One is broadcasting intermittently right now," Jenny said.

"And we must have one person on duty to repair them at all times," Commander Aarons said.

I thought for a moment. Sure, it was dangerous. So was breathing, if you did it long enough. And Ishi hadn't been afraid.

"Sounds reasonable to me," I said. "I'll be glad to switch over from Monitoring, if you need me."

"Ah. Good." Commander Aarons stood up. "Best of luck." He shook my hand. It gave me a warm friendly feeling.

When we were out of the office, and Dad had gone back to Monitoring I turned to Jenny and said, "Was this your idea?"

"Mine? Don't be silly. Commander Aarons called me in just a few minutes before you. He wanted to know if I would mind working with you."

"Okay. Sorry. I guess I'm just a little edgy today. The last twenty-four hours hasn't done me a whole lot of good."

Jenny looked sad. "I know what you mean."

We walked down to the student rec center to get something to eat. We had to stand in line.

"I think we ought to go down to the main bay and begin going over your shuttle," Jenny said.

"Huh?"

"Well, you're going to have to learn how to operate it sometime. I know you've done some simple piloting, but—"

"You mean you're supposed to teach me?"

"Who else?"

"Well . . ."

"Say, is there some reason you don't want to work with me?"

"Uh, no," I lied.

In the back of my mind I was thinking about Zak's theory about what living so close together in the Can had done to us. It felt right. Jenny was like the rest of the girls

I knew. Buddies, I guess you'd say. I could see she was pretty and smart and reliable, sure. And I'd been thinking of her that way for as long as I could remember. But now I wanted something else.

Something had started me thinking. Maybe it had been Zak and his comical Rebecca and Isaac, lurching around and pounding away at each other. I felt like a dummy, a goody-goody boy stuck out here around Jupiter, while back on Earth a guy my age knew about women and how to treat them. Well, that was going to change. But until I could figure out how to do that, I didn't want to be all palsy with Jenny. Not when I could maybe be something more . . .

"Hey, are you paying attention?" she said.

"Huh? Oh yeah. Look, let's get this training over with, huh?"

She looked at me curiously. "You seem a little nervous about something, Matt."

"Naw, I'm okay."

"You sure?"

"Sure I'm sure."

Jenny shrugged.

"It could not be because you are afraid, of course," a deep voice said.

I turned. Yuri had filled in the line behind us.

"Get away, Sagdaeff," I said.

"Don't be silly, Yuri," Jenny said. "Matt isn't afraid."

"Oh, I don't know about that. He did not react very well under stress on Ganymede."

"How would you like a flat nose?" I said.

"Ah ha, threatening violence. The last resort of the incompetent. I wonder what Commander Aarons would think if you were to hit me in public?"

"Let's find out," I said, raising my arms.

"Yuri! Matt! Stop it. Yuri, go away. You started it."

"I merely came over to congratulate Matt on his new position."

"How did you know?" I said.

"Rumors, rumors. And I happened to be talking to the Commander's secretary when she was typing up the change of status report." Yuri smiled coldly at me.

Jenny said, "Yuri . . ."

"All right, I am leaving." He walked away.

"What was *that* all about?" Jenny said. "Did it have anything to do with what Commander Aarons said?"

So I told her about Ganymede and the air hose. It was already getting to be an old story.

"I see," Jenny said, thoughtfully chewing a sandwich. (By this time we had been through the line.) "That explains a lot of Yuri's behavior."

"It does?"

"Of course. Look," she said, tossing her head to get some brown curls out of her eyes, "it must have been a hard thing for Yuri to have to admit to himself that he made a big mistake with the air hose. It hurt him."

"Hurt his ego, you mean. It makes a big target."

"All right, it damaged his self-image. He is miffed. And he's taking it out on you."

"Why me? *I* saved him."

"You saw him make the mistake, too."

"This sounds pretty twisted to me."

"Maybe it is, but *some*thing must be making him act this way."

"Let's make a deal," I said, patting her hand. "You don't psychoanalyze me and I promise not to run berserk. Okay?" I decided not to go into Zak's theory about Yuri, even though I was sure it was true. What could be gained?

"I didn't know you were about to."

"Well, I might if people keep giving me advice. Come on, let's get to work. Is the *Ballerina* ready?"

She got up, straightening her red blouse, and said, "Yes, but that's not the shuttle we'll be using to train you."

"Oh? Ishi's then. What's its name?"

"He never gave it one," she said as we left the cafeteria. "It was entered in the log by its inventory number."

"I'll name it myself, then."

"What?"

"*Roadhog*," I said.

We suited up and cycled through the Can's main lock. The vehicle bay is just outside the lock, but the bay isn't a particular room you can point at—it's simply the big open space in the hollow part of the Can. All the small-sized vehicles are kept there and secured at the axis with a network of elastic tie-lines, to be sure they don't bang into each other. All along the inner face of the Can are slots for berthing; when a vehicle needs to be fueled or worked over, it's pulled into a berth. Otherwise it's moored a good distance from the Can's skin, in high vacuum that does it no harm.

Jenny and I clipped on to the mooring lines and pushed off. After a moment of coasting I turned so my feet pointed toward the shuttle and squirted my attitude jets. That slowed me to a crawl and I unclipped from the line just as the shuttle swelled up to block my view of the opposite inner wall of the Can. I landed, catlike.

I swung around, found a pipe and attached my own suit tie-line to it. The shuttles are all different: each one was thrown together with whatever spare parts came to hand. The *Roadhog*—I'd silently christened it the moment my glove touched the pipe—looked like a conglomerate of castoffs until you studied the structure.

It was a bit like an automobile chassis, all bones and no skin. The pilot was belted into a couch at the center. He was surrounded by pipes and struts and fuel tanks, without having his view obscured. A small yellow ion-engine was mounted behind him. The whole thing was lumpy but balanced; spacecraft have to be stable.

I glided over to the pilot's couch and perched on top of the backrest. Around us, never closer than twenty yards, were other craft. A few had their running lights on; they were being checked over or preparing to go out. A big tube-shaped cargo hauler was moored right above us. Beyond that the gray water-shield plugged the bore of the Can. Below I could see someone using a cutting torch, its flame a sharp, fierce blue diamond.

I heard a faint *clank* as Jenny bumped into the shuttle. She secured her suit safety line and came swarming over to me.

She touched helmets. "You know how to use the air tanks on this one, don't you?"

"Sure."

"Take us over there, then," she said, pointing to Berth H.

I buckled myself into the pilot couch and reached out gingerly for the controls. You don't use an ion engine inside the Can's bay, or even nearby if you can help it. The backwash can knock a man head over heels a hundred meters away, or snarl mooring lines. So I gently thumbed in the override on the shuttle's air tanks, switched them over to the pipe system that led to the little maneuvering jets at the rear, and reached for the release button.

"Forgotten anything?" Jenny said lightly.

"Huh?"

"Our mooring lines."

"Oh." I felt my face go red. I unbuckled and glided around the four corners of the *Roadhog*, unhooking the elastic lines. They're on retrieval coils, so as soon as I let go a line it retracted toward the axis.

I sat back down in the couch. "All cleared, Captain."

She didn't say anything. I carefully bled a little air into the pipes and felt a satisfying tug as we got under way. I gave us little bursts of air to maneuver around the cargo hauler overhead and cut in the gyros to keep us from tumbling.

We inched our way across the bay. I got back into the practice of looking in three different directions at once; my neck started to ache. Human beings are built for navigating in two dimensions; our eyes are set in a line parallel to the ground, suitable for chasing wildebeests. Outer space takes some getting used to. Even after you've trained your stomach to stop pushing the panic button when you're in no-g conditions, you have to keep reminding yourself that up and down are just as important as sideways. The adjustment is never perfect, because you're trying to learn a set of reflexes your body just wasn't programmed to take. That's why no-g maneuvering takes a lot of energy—you're fighting yourself all the way, whether you know it or not. I suppose that's why kids like me are a little better at no-g work and don't tire so fast; our reflexes aren't totally "set" yet.

Berth H was a square-mouthed tube with bright lights lining the inside. I edged the *Roadhog* into the slot that brought us to a stop nearly perfectly; we couldn't have been moving faster than a meter per second when we bumped into the buffer pads at the end.

Jenny patted me on the shoulder and bounded away to fasten mooring lines.

I felt good. I had proved that I could still handle a shuttlecraft, despite being out of practice. And most of all, I was out in space again. It had been too long.

That was the high point. The next five hours were something less than gratifying. Jenny took me over the *Roadhog* inch by inch, making me learn every valve and meter and strut on the contraption. I had forgotten a lot; the rest I hadn't learned at all.

She made me draw a flowchart for the air pipes, after letting me inspect the *Roadhog* for five minutes. I thought I'd figured it out. When she handed the clipboard back to me, covered with red marks, I found out that I had gotten everything exactly backwards.

I checked out the works: ring laser gyros, radio, first aid, fuel feeds, hauling collars, repair kit, spare parts, search lights, electrical system, navigation, backup systems, vector integrator—you name it, I had to find it, see if it worked, explain how I would repair it if it didn't, and relate it to all the other systems it meshed with.

"Do you think you're familiar with these things now?" Jenny said.

"I'm surprised you don't have me kiss each one individually," I said. She grinned at me. I grinned back; a lock of hair had curled down between her eyes—she couldn't reach it, of course, in a space suit—and I wondered why I hadn't realized before how pretty she was.

My old romanticism again. The people I respected most were the ones who could do things. Most girls didn't fit in that category and I—ambitious Matt Bohles—looked down my nose at them. What good is a girl who is just an ornament?

For some reason I had included Jenny in that group, too. These last few hours had proven me wrong. I was intrigued. Jenny was something special.

"Do you feel ready to take her out?" Jenny said. I

blinked; I had been staring at her moodily, thinking, for the last minute.

"The *Roadhog* is not a her, it's a him," I said.

"Ships are always feminine," she said. "There are female roadhogs, too. So what's your answer?"

"Alone?"

"Of course not. I'll be holding your hot little hand all the way." She looked at her watch. "The round trip should take about thirteen hours. It's too late to leave today."

"What's the trip for?"

"Satellite Fourteen. A circuit component is on the fritz and the Faraday cup doesn't give reasonable readings."

I shrugged and then remembered that in a suit the gesture was invisible. "Fine. Tomorrow morning, then, huh?"

Chapter 10

That night we had one of our godawful Socials. The psychers have this theory: As kids approach the teenage years, there's this natural tendency to clump. Girls in one group over here, and the boys in that gang over there. You can't get them together in the right kind of social way without an effort, they say. So every month they have a Social and every teenager in the Can has to come. There's no option. No begging off with a cold, no conflicting job. *Nothing* will get you off the hook.

I got there as late as I could. Everybody does. Good music was floating out of the corners of the H-deck rec room. A couple of adults were welcoming kids as they came in the door. The adults were basically good people, warm and understanding and always willing to talk to you. Everybody knows they're part-time "adolescent specialists" —you can look it up in the Can work chart—but that's okay, because that's what they're honestly interested in. It's no fake. "Good evening, Matt," Mr. Neugyen murmured to me. "I believe the correct theme for tonight is a quiet, reflective time." He gestured to the rec room. "We are all saddened by the passing of Ishi. But to reaffirm our—"

"Yeah, you're right," I said, mostly to cut him off.

Dr. Matonin turned to me. "I know it has affected you greatly," she said.

I scuffed one shoe into the other. "Uh huh." They were only trying to help, and they were right, but I didn't want to talk about it. "Uh, I think I'll get something to drink," I said, and moved off with a kind of phony smile.

It was just like every other Social. A knot of boys were talking, occasionally letting out a bark of laughter. The girls sat around low toadstool-shaped tables, the kind you can knock a drink off of with your knee if you're not careful. They looked bored and uncomfortable. Just a few hours earlier we'd all seen them in jumpers or skinsuits or overalls. Now they had dresses and long floaty skirts. And they'd done something to themselves. I mean, we'd been seeing the same dresses for years, redone to keep up with Earthside styles. But tonight the girls managed to look different—softer and curvier and sexier somehow. I don't know how they did it.

I went over the punchbowl and got a cup of the usual yellowish stuff. No alcohol in it, of course. Nothing more exotic, either. I'd never heard of anybody in the Can using any of the mild euphorics, such as cannabis or Lucogen. Those are legal on Earth, but reality-twisting isn't allowed out here.

"Hey, got one for me?" Jenny said at my elbow.

I handed her my cup. "Oh, I didn't see you." I poured myself another.

"Or didn't try to, ummmm?"

"Aw, come on."

"Well, I wondered if there was some reason. Do you realize that you *never* approach a girl at these things?" She sipped her punch, holding it in two hands and peered over the cup at me.

"Let's be precise," I said. "I don't very often, okay, but not *never*. I . . . well, there's something I don't like about these things."

"They're not the greatest," she admitted.

"Why can't we have square dances instead?"

She shrugged. "Dr. Matonin says these are part of the, the socialization program."

"That's right," Dr. Matonin said. "Socialization." She had come over at the sound of her name. We smiled and exchanged a few pleasantries. Then I looked straight at her and said, "Look, we already *know* each other. Why do we have to go through these dances?"

Dr. Matonin has a motherly look and smiles a lot. It's impossible not to like her. Her face crinkled with concern. "Social dancing is the way boys and girls learn to, ah, interact with each other."

"We interact each day," Jenny pointed out.

"I mean in a context that will develop and grow in later years. We want to bring you youngsters together in a way that will break down the tendency you have to avoid the other sex during adolescence."

"But we get along fine," I said.

"In a more sophisticated way, I mean, Matt."

By that I guessed she meant the long ritual of dating and engagement and marriage, with a dollop of sex thrown in somewhere along the way to keep your interest up. Playing the game, Zak called it.

"Why can't they be square dances, then?" Jenny asked. "We used to have those and they were fun."

I nodded. I liked square dancing. It wasn't such a hassle. You could wear anything you felt like. That usually meant the guys wore whatever they had on at the moment, and maybe half the girls did the same. The other girls came in skirts. For square dancing the skirts made sense—they were cooler. In fact, it always seemed too bad that boys couldn't wear something like a skirt, too. I mean, to have some freedom of dress.

"I agree, they *were* fun." Dr. Matonin's face lit up. "But you young men and women are getting older and it is time to move on to other kinds of, ah, socialization processes."

"Like this?" I waved a hand at the decorations and subdued lighting.

"Yes, indeed. This seems to us to be what is needed."

"Needed by who?" Jenny asked.

"By the less mature among you. They do not easily make contact with the other sex. There *are* shy people, you know—they're not all like *you*, Matt," she said merrily.

I stared at her. She's a tremendously bright fusion physicist, sure. But she didn't seem to see that I felt awkward at these Socials, just like everybody else. I had a sudden moment of insight there, catching a glimpse of how other people saw me. A little jolt of unreality.

I was kind of brash and self-confident. I knew that. But underneath I had doubts and uncertainties. There were moments when I was nervous or shy or afraid to say things. But from what Dr. Matonin said, I guessed that nobody saw me clearly at those moments. They didn't think that a kid who was good at his job and pretty fast with his mouth could have any problems. Well, I had news for them.

"But, but," Jenny said, "there's more social contact at *any*thing else than *here*." She gestured and we looked around. Sure enough, girls were still looking bored and guys were against one wall, muttering in subdued voices. Nobody was dancing.

"Well, it's early yet," Dr. Matonin said. "There's something you older teens have got to understand, as well," she went on seriously. "These dances are basically for the sake of the girls. They like them, even if perhaps a few of the older girls don't." A nod at Jenny. "They like a chance to dress up and show off. They like making their own special clothes."

"We could wear them anywhere we wanted. Not only to dances."

Dr. Matonin nodded slightly. "But you *don't*. You see, Jenny, the Can is a very special kind of environment. We don't dress or act the way people back on Earth do. But Mr. Neugyen and I and the others are trying to make these Socials as much as possible like the way things are on Earth. This is the way life *is*, Jenny. It's not all work crews and astronomy and computers. And we had better remember that. We will all have to go back and live on

Earth, someday, and we will have trouble adjusting. And you will have the worst time of all, because you've spent almost all of your lives in the Can."

"Ummm," Jenny murmured in the way that meant she wasn't convinced.

"So go ahead, get on out there," Dr. Matonin said brightly, gently taking each of us by the elbow and steering us onto the dance floor. "And enjoy yourselves."

I'm no smoothie, but I can negotiate a simple box step without breaking an ankle. I took Jenny in my arms and we danced through several numbers. It wasn't bad. I liked the smell of her, a kind of rich fragrance that blotted out the rec room and the clumps of guys and the syrupy music. Jenny smiled and I held her closer and it was not bad at all. It still felt phony, but I managed to forget about that part of it.

We talked some more about what Dr. Matonin said. Jenny didn't think *any* of the girls really liked the Socials, despite Dr. Matonin's theory.

Jenny and I danced on. I saw Zak wandering around the place, cup in hand. When we all took a break Jenny went off to the john. I wandered over to where Zak was leaning in a corner. He's the Can's Number One word magician in ordinary conversation, but I've noticed that he doesn't stand out much at the Socials. He hardly ever dances and he doesn't say much.

"What're you doing hiding over here?" I asked.

"Passing the time."

"Eyeing the girls, you mean. Why not ask one to dance? They don't bite. Not often, anyway."

"I'm sizing them up. Picking out the target."

"Target for what?"

"Remember Ishi's Lady X?"

"Oh."

"She's got to be in this room. Right in front of us." He gestured dramatically.

"Maybe."

"No maybes, she's *here*. Unless she was some twenty-year-old." His eyes widened at the implication. "Say, you don't suppose he might've—"

"Look, who can tell? That information's lost."

"Ah, my friend, but the Lady X is not. All I have to do is find her."

"I think you're looking at this the wrong way."

"How so?"

"It's not a rabbit hunt. I mean, you don't just put her in your sights and whammo, there you are."

"Why not?"

"Well . . ." I wasn't sure quite what I *did* mean. "Look, it's got to mean something more than that."

He smirked. "Old romantic Matt."

"Maybe I've just got higher standards, huh?" I growled.

Zak shrugged. "We were discussing technique, not principles."

"No, look, I don't even think your approach will work. If you zoom in on some poor girl, right away she's going to suspect what you're after. She'll turn off, fast."

Zak shrugged again. "We'll see, we'll see."

I pitied the girl Zak came on with. He'd stand offshore and try the familiar verbal barrage to soften her up. Then he'd follow it with a vigorous assault on the beaches. She'd push him right back into the sea. I was pretty sure of that. Still . . . I looked around at the hundred or so kids in the rec hall. Somewhere in here was Lady X, Zak was probably right about that. Which one? Even if I figured out who she was, there were always some goddamn chaperones around. It did make you think, though . . .

I shook myself. *Come on Matt.*

"Hey, isn't that—hot damn, it is!" Zak cried, and then chuckled.

I looked toward the door. Yuri was standing there, halfway in. He was wearing some breeches that looked like leather, and a flowery, ruffled shirt, with cuffs that flared open. "Geez, what's *that?*" I said in wonder.

Then I noticed that a slightly shorter man was gesturing for Yuri to come on in. Yuri's father. I'd seen him around.

Zak said, "Looks like some costume from the Middle Ages."

Yuri's father called, "Dr. Matonin, I propose a new event for these Socials." He smiled broadly and tugged

Yuri through the hatchway. By now everybody had noticed Yuri's getup and the whole room was quiet. "A traditional Ukranian dance, the *savabodnaya*. I think the children will enjoy it just as much as your more western dances."

Dr. Sagdaeff looked a little red in the nose and he was perspiring freely. I guessed maybe he'd had a little bit to drink. Yuri stood beside him, looking like he'd rather be a thousand klicks away. In fact, being dead wouldn't be a bad alternative, either.

"Well, I suppose later we can try a few steps," Dr. Matonin said diplomatically. "This *is* a social dancing occasion, but . . ."

"Yuri here, I had him put on the traditional costume. Brought all the way from the Ukraine, it is."

"So I see."

"It will help to get in the mood. Show her, Yuri."

Yuri bit his lip. He stood frozen, the breeches too tight for him. His eyes raced around the room and his face was red. "Papa. I . . ."

"Yuri! Dance!" His father's voice was suddenly harsh.

"Papa—"

"Come!" Dr. Sagdaeff began clapping loudly and stomping one foot a quarter-note off the claps. It made a pleasant contrapuntal effect. "Come!"

Yuri started to do a little jogging dance. The steps were intricate. The rhythm picked you up, though. It was a good dancing beat, I found my own foot tapping along.

It was fine as long as you didn't look at Yuri. The big lug bounced around, feet busy, face rigid. You could tell he was embarrassed. On somebody smaller the costume would've looked odd, but interesting, and maybe exotic. On Yuri it just looked funny.

Jenny came over and gave me a sidelong glance, grimacing.

Zak whispered, "Good grief, it's agonizing to watch."

"Yes," Jenny said. "How can a father make a public exhibit of his son that way?"

"He must have Yuri on pretty tight reins," I murmured.

"Looks like it," Jenny agreed. "That might explain a lot."

I said, "Like what?"

"What makes Yuri run, Matt-o," Zak put in.

"You mean his father?"

"Might be," Jenny said. "Something's driving Yuri to compete. A father who can force you to, well—"

Zak supplied, "Make a fool of yourself in public."

"Yes. Well, a father like that can egg you on to succeed, win every contest, be the best on every test. This certainly fits the pattern and helps explain it."

"Shrewd analysis," Zak said.

I thought about it. It didn't make Yuri any more likable, but maybe it did clear up some mystery about why he was always such a dorp. Parents can do you a lot of damage.

By now Yuri was grimacing and glaring around at everybody, as if daring them to say something. His father was gaily clapping and stomping, oblivious to it all. He probably was remembering some childhood dance of his own, back in the sunny-speckled wheat fields of the Ukraine. It didn't seem to matter to him that Yuri didn't share his fondness.

Jenny murmured, "That's part of the Yuri riddle, all right. But y'know, sometimes I think guys who are big bruisers act that way because that's what we expect of them. There's some truth to that, too."

I frowned, trying to puzzle that one out. Jenny sees these things clearer than I do. Hell, I was beginning to think *every*body did.

Dr. Matonin raised her voice. "Dr. Sagdaeff? Dr. Sagdaeff!" The clapping slowed and stopped. Yuri quit dancing with obvious relief. "I'm sure we would all be interested in learning such a dance . . . later, after we have had some social dancing. We thank you very much for the demonstration. If you could help us learn it later?" Then she smoothly guided some couples into a Latin American number as the canned music swelled up again.

Jenny said reflectively. "Actually, it is an interesting looking dance."

"Kind of like square dancing," I said, "but harder."

"Ummmm," she mused. "Look at Yuri. Does *he* look awkward."

Yuri was standing around, looking at the couples. His peasant costume or whatever it was had looked okay while he danced and while he moved around. Standing still, he just looked silly. "Yeah," I said.

"You know," she said, "your smirk doesn't have to be *that* superior."

"C'mon, let's dance," I said. But she was right. It did feel good to gloat.

Chapter 11

I got up early the next day and beat Jenny down to the vehicle bay. I fooled around, poking my nose into some other ships moored nearby, until I got a call over suit radio. I turned and saw her kicking off from the lock.

"My Captain cometh," I said.

"Not me, kid. You're in charge on this one."

"What about *Roadhog*? Is she fueled? He, I mean."

"Don't fight it. The *Roadhog* is a she. And of course she's fueled. *I'm* not sloppy at maintenance."

We coasted into Berth G, freed the lines, and Jenny gracefully swung into the pilot's couch. She called in to the bridge and had an updated flight plan transmitted to the shuttle computer's memory. Then I took over. I ran quickly through the standard checklist. Jenny sat on the flat bench next to the couch, buckled herself in and gave me the high sign.

I backed us cautiously out of the berth and brought the nose up to a point at the "top" of the Can. We still carried the angular velocity of the Can, so I gave the lateral jets a burst. We backed away from the Can's inner wall. The Can appeared to spin faster and faster and I thumbed in more side thrust.

I gave *Roadhog* one burst of LOX through the rear jets and coasted for the top of the Can in one long, clean line. We glided by the shadowy shapes of parked craft, safety neons splashing pools of light over them. The Can pinwheeled about us. Viewports passed, glowing softly. In one a woman looked up at her skylight and saw us. She waved. Jenny waved back. The interior of the Can, with its soft yellow glow, already seemed far away.

We passed the *Sagan*. Thick hoses sprouted from her water tanks and snaked into sockets on the Can's axis. Above, the pancake sac of water reflected Jove's amber light on its mottled plastic skin. As we reached the top of the Can I bled out a stream of air from the decelerating jets and we came to a halt.

The water shields are held by a few mooring lines, stationary above the Can itself. There's about fifty meters clearance between the Can top and the pancake, enough for us to slip out. The shields are only moved to let out a big cruiser ship like the *Sagan*; otherwise they sit there, blocking high energy electrons. I turned us so we pointed out, between the Can and the gray water-shield. Jupiter peeked over the rim as we cleared the top of the Can. It was a crescent; the Can was moving sunward in its orbit.

The shuttle shifted and murmured under me. The computer program was taking over. I punched the release button on the small control board and instantly felt a slight thrust. The ion engine had cut in. It made no noise; it's a low-impulse system.

We went straight up, away from the Lab, as though the Can was a cannon and we had been shot out of it. I was looking at Jupiter through the spaces in the *Roadhog*'s floor.

"Hey," I said, "we're heading due north."

"Most observant. We're going into a polar orbit."

"Satellite Fourteen is in a polar orbit?"

"Nearly. Monitoring and Astrophysics are making it pretty popular. Satellite Fourteen is in an eccentric orbit that takes it in close to Jupiter's poles."

"So it gets the best data on the storms?"

"That's what I hear. I just fix 'em, I don't try to understand 'em. Look, you can see the storms now."

I followed her pointing finger. Near the north pole of Jupiter the bands broke and eddied and lost some of their bright orange color. I could make out tiny whirlpools that churned up the edges of the bands.

"Is a storm brewing?" I said.

"No, we're seeing the last gasp of one that peaked five days ago. Astrophysics said they didn't think another would come along for a while yet, but that's only a guess."

"What's the radiation level like during the storm?"

"High. Higher than they've ever seen before, Astrophysics says. Why, worried?"

"Yup. I'm too young to be broiled in an electron shower. Are the shielding fields on?" I looked at my control panel. Everything glowed green.

"Yes, they went on automatically when we left the Lab. Don't worry."

"Don't mind me, I'm a natural worrier." I looked around at the superconducting bars that ring the *Roadhog*, though of course you can't *see* the magnetic fields they produce. Those bars were all that kept Jupiter's Van Allen belts from frying us alive.

Radiation is a subtle thing. You can't see it or taste it, but those little electrons and protons can fry you in an hour. They are why the Lab wasn't orbited in close to Jupiter.

Earth and Jupiter have one big thing in common: radiation belts. A man named Van Allen discovered them back in the early Space Age, around Earth. A little later Jupiter turned out to have them, too. Mars doesn't, nor Venus, nor Mercury. Reason: no magnetic fields. Earth and Jupiter generate big magnetic fields around them, and those fields trap high-energy particles that the Sun throws out.

They're called belts because that's what they look like—big doughnuts around Jupiter and Earth, many planetary radii in diameter. The Lab had to be located out beyond the worst part of that doughnut or we'd be cooked with radiation. Even so, the Lab has water tanks that line the outside of the Can and stop incoming particles before they can reach the living quarters.

The *Roadhog* hasn't got that mass. It's a shuttle, engineered for speed and economy. So you don't go out in it during radiation storms.

Extra mass might have stopped the pellet that killed Ishi. Maybe there was an argument for putting shielding around the shuttles. Magnetic fields don't affect pieces of rock, because the rock is electrically neutral; only encasing a shuttle in heavy walls would make it really safe.

But I wasn't planning on applying for an insurance policy, anyway. I stopped brooding about Ishi and turned to Jenny.

"What's wrong with Satellite Fourteen anyway?"

"Here," she said, handing me a clipboard with a maze of circuit diagrams on it. "A problem for the student."

I found the circuit component that was fouling up pretty fast. The tough part was the Faraday cup.

The cup on most satellites, including fourteen, is a simple affair. It has an electrostatically charged grid open to the space around the satellite. Any charged particle that wanders by can be attracted by the grid. When it is, it picks up some added velocity and overshoots the grid—goes right through it—and runs smack into a collector. The process builds up a voltage across a capacitor. Every so often a watch officer in Monitoring—somebody like me—will call for a count from the satellite. The capacitor will be discharged, the voltage measured, and a little arithmetic gives the number of particles (usually electrons) the cup captured.

Satellite Fourteen's cup wasn't working. I had my own idea why. I didn't think they were well designed.

"Hey, look," Jenny said. I looked down, through the *Roadhog's* floor. A brownish whirlpool, thick with blotches of red, was churning in the clouds below.

"That one reminds me of the Red Spot," I said.

"I've never seen anything like it before. Odd color."

"There are some funny things going on in that atmosphere. Old Jove is putting on a show for us."

"I wonder why."

"Come back in ten years. Maybe we'll know then."

The nice thing about having somebody along on a trip is the reassurance you get. It's easy, out in space, to get swallowed up in the vastness of everything. Being able to talk to somebody brings things back into perspective.

So we chattered away. I'd never spent that much time alone with Jenny, and I found out a lot of things about her I didn't know. What I saw I liked.

That's the way it went, for six hours. Yes, six. Jupiter

is *big*. The *Roadhog* pushed steadily at our backs and took us upward, toward the north pole, so we could match orbits with Satellite Fourteen.

We spotted a tiny glimmering dot on our left while the *Roadhog* was making final adjustments with its maneuvering jets. It grew rapidly: a silvery ball sprouting antennas and small attitude jets. It was one of the older satellites, which probably explained why it failed.

Jenny stayed in the shuttle while I coasted across to the satellite. It was basketball-sized, its shiny skin pitted. I pulled out several shelves of circuitry, disconnected the Faraday cup and went back to Jenny.

We both looked over the parts and discussed what to do about them. That's the advantage of sending out a human being, rather than relying on multiple backup systems—the space around Jupiter is unknown, and no engineer back on Earth can predict what will happen to his pet gadget after a few years of pounding from high-energy electrons, dust and micrometeorites. In jargonese they call it "failure to allow for contingencies."

We made some repairs on the circuitry. Working in gloves is awkward and even slipping microchip decks snugly into place can be difficult. We both had modified our suits for the work. We had a big flap on the chest that pulled down, revealing a big adhesive patch. Pull the flap down, stick the securing tab on a knee, and there you have half a square meter of microhooks. They'll hang onto anything until you give it a good tug. If you've ever chased a lost thermocouple over a cubic klick of space, because you let go of it for a nanosecond or two, you'd appreciate an adhesive patch. Some techs have them on their arms, legs, every place they can see and reach.

After the standard repairs, I looked at the cup. It was a mess. Intermittent shorts, crappy signal characteristics. I didn't think much of the design, either. Looked like ancient history. "Maybe we should keep it as it is," I suggested. "For a museum piece." Under Jenny's schoolmarm eye I took it out, worked the replacement in, checked connections, and then ran a few tests on the rest of the oversized silver basketball. Everything looked okay. I coasted back.

"Not bad," Jenny said. "You only took fifty-three minutes."

On the long arc back we ate some squeeze-soup and tried to relax. I was tired. There is a kind of tension that comes from carrying out delicate operations in zero-g. Your muscles do far more than is necessary, without your even knowing it. Only later do you feel the aches seep into your joints.

Satellite Fourteen was one of the three satellites that looped in close over the pole, to get readings where the magnetic fields are strongest. We got a good view of the Great White Oval, a mixmaster of colors inside a glaring white swirl. As we watched it Jenny and I started to talk. The grand dance of Jove went on beneath, so vivid and alive you felt as if you could reach out and touch it. Somebody had called it "the greatest found art object in the solar system," back in the twentieth century. Dead right. God's palette. And as we stared at the hypnotic technicolor swirl, Jenny and I began to talk, really talk. And what came out was a lot of the things I'd always thought but never said.

I told her about the way the whole social thing looks to me—and to a lot of boys growing up. We're driven by a big urge—*get laid!* the hormones sing. But everyone says *no, you're too young. You'll get in trouble.* You sort of expect your parents and The System to keep saying *no*—they always do; they're cautious. So you discount that. But the girls say it, too. That's because they've been sold a bill of goods, just like us. They have everybody wagging fingers at them, saying *Watch out! Don't give in. Don't even think of giving in. You're not ready for it, emotionally ready. And you could get pregnant.* And they're right, in a way. Girls pay the bigger price. Their whole growing-up process is filled with fears of things that might happen to them. Boys never have to worry about getting pregnant. Or raped. And suppose you're a thirteen-year-old girl and you decide you're going to have sex no matter what anybody says? If you do anything to prevent pregnancy, you're in trouble. The doctor tells your parents and then *they* come down on you. And if you *don't* see the doctor, then maybe you wind up having a baby or getting an abortion. Some choice, uh?

I could see all that. Girls had it hard. Maybe harder than we did. Or maybe the trouble was just different. Boys had this drive and it seemed powerful as hell. You thought about it all the time.

Jenny said, well, sure, she thought about sex; but not all the time. Maybe for boys it was different. For girls, sex was an expression of something else a lot of the time. Of affection. Or a sense of self-esteem (I'm a woman; somebody wants me). Or sometimes as a reward to the boy for something. And a girl sees images of women all over the place while she's growing up—magazines, 3D ads. And they're all actresses' pinups, beautifully groomed and busty and leggy. "Most girls get a kind of inferiority complex out of all that," Jenny said. "So sex gets to be a thing you're kind of shy of, because compared to those gorgeous women on 3D, you're not so much. How could any man desire *you*?"

There were two reactions to this, she murmured, making a sour expression. A girl could go out and try to prove herself—and run all the risks I had been talking about. Or she could just hang back, shy. Neither solution really worked. It just delayed the real problem, which was coming to grips with your own personality, who you really *were*.

Maybe so, I said, but it seemed to me we *all* got wounded. After a while of frustration, a guy got to seeing girls as the enemy. *They* were the ones doing the rejecting, the ones who were holding out. *They* could come across if they wanted to. So a guy builds up this resentment of women, and he keeps it. Even after he's got things sort of straightened out, there are always those years when he was a teenager and every hand was turned against what his body told him to do. Walking wounded, yeah. A guy doesn't forget.

Jenny said softly, "I think I see what you mean. The training we get from our parents and others—it makes us think the other sex is different, an enemy. Sure, maybe they don't intend it to have that effect. But it *does*."

"Right."

"We're all victims, then."

"Yeah. I can understand how things got this way. . ."

"Especially out here in the Can."

"Right. But that doesn't mean I have to like it."

She nodded solemnly and looked at me. "I don't either."

The talk sort of dribbled off. We started to get tired. We buckled in and got some hours of zero-g sleep.

When the bridge of the Can called, I woke up. I felt pretty well rested. The Can was already a glowing dot, spinning patiently.

I jockeyed the *Roadhog* into the bay and we both did the refueling; it was beginning to look like we would make a good team. Most shuttle hops weren't so long and one operator would do, but on jobs like this one the bridge liked two pilots along.

I felt good. It seemed like something to celebrate, so I invited Jenny for a drink—a *real* one, not a milkshake.

I unsuited, went through the 'fresher—ever smell someone who's been working in a space suit for over thirteen hours?—and waited for Jenny in the tube outside the women's area. I had planned on taking her to the small officer's bar on one of the outer levels, where a big 3D screen gives views of Earth and I thought we wouldn't meet anyone we knew. It was 20:00 hours, ship's time, well past the cocktail hour.

I had just leaned against the wall when Zak came loping along, panting.

"I figured you'd be here," he gasped. "Want—wanted to catch you."

"What for?"

"Commander Aarons called a shipwide meeting, it's starting right now. I thought you'd probably missed the announcement while you were coming inside."

Jenny appeared. "What announcement? What is it?"

"Come on," Zak said.

"I think we ought to go," I said apologetically. Jenny and I looked at each other. We shrugged. "A little later, maybe . . ."

Jenny smiled and nodded. We followed Zak, who was already walking away. I felt bad about interrupting our little private party. Alcohol holds no fascination for me— I've had plenty of chances to drink at home, so it's nothing new—but there is something about the rituals of drinking that can cement new ties, formalize a relationship. And I suppose I wanted to mark the occasion. I wanted to make a bench mark that said, here is when I opened my eyes a little, and saw her clearly for the first time.

Zak told us about a flurry of rumors that had run around the Lab during the day, most of them contradictory. I half-listened on the way to the auditorium. The bowl was nearly filled. The 3D cameras were operating, so that people who couldn't leave their posts could listen in. We found three seats together on the very last row.

The auditorium buzzed with speculation. I spotted Mom and Dad sitting together, the Motos, and several others. The lights dimmed slightly. People stopped chattering and Commander Aarons walked to the podium at center stage. He seemed smaller than I remembered him, and awfully tired. He reached up and nervously plucked at his moustache before speaking.

"It is my duty to make a grave announcement. Two hours ago I received word from the Executive Council of the International Space Administration. For the last several weeks the Council has deliberated on the future course of research and exploration throughout the solar system.

"The discussions were extensive. Plans for construction of the first unmanned probes to the nearby stars were even considered; the Council elected to set aside such a program for the foreseeable future.

"As many of you may have suspected, it was an order of the Council that delayed the departure of the *Argosy*. I did not know why until this evening.

"We are all aware—however divorced we may be from our home planet—that the economic crisis there is steadily worsening. Overpopulation has not been solved. Raw materials are running low, despite the self-supporting mines in the asteroid belt. Gradually the 'extras' are being whittled away.

"I am afraid the Council has decided that it is the Laboratory's turn to be trimmed. No, no—" he looked toward the top of the bowl, directly at me—"that is far too mild a word. The Council has informed me . . . that all research operations here and on Ganymede are to be ended. The Laboratory is finished."

Chapter 12

Suddenly everybody was talking at once. The Commander let the noise build for a moment and then cut it off by raising his hand.

"The *Argosy* will leave Earth orbit within the hour. It is flying empty; none of the cargo we asked for is aboard, nor are food supplements. The Council has given orders that the Laboratory be stripped of useful scientific instruments. All personnel are to return to Earth on the *Argosy*."

"Impossible!" someone down front shouted.

The Commander shook his head. "It is not. The Council sent detailed plans for departure. If we squeeze, we can make it."

"But why? Why so sudden?" the same person said again.

Commander Aarons relaxed his stance and leaned slightly against the podium. He seemed glad that the formal announcement was over and he could talk normally. "We've always known that there are factions on the Council who oppose space research farther away than Luna. I believe since the recent elections they are in the driver's seat."

Mr. Jablons stood up. "Commander, we have as much patience as anyone. We all know ISA has been trying to nickel and dime us to death for years, with little cuts here and there. But this isn't a cut, it's a hangman's noose. I say we should fight it!"

"Right!"

"I'm with Jablons!"

"Very fine, gentlemen," the Commander said. "What do you propose?"

"Shoot the Council!"

Commander Aarons smiled wryly. "Impractical, I am afraid. Anyone else?"

Mrs. Moto stood up. "We are citizens of many different countries. Could we appeal through our geographical representatives?"

"We are only a few more than twelve hundred people, Madam," Commander Aarons said. "We carry very little political clout."

"Senator Davidson has always supported the Lab. We can appeal to him," a voice said.

A man stood and waved for attention from the Commander. When he got it he said, "Judging from a few hints in the legislative reports we get sandwiched into the news from Earth, Senator Davidson fought for us and lost. He has relinquished his position on the Advisory Board." The Commander nodded. "Anyway, a senator is a creature half-man and half-horse. Normally the top half is a man. You can't expect them to set sail against the prevailing winds."

Some people nodded; others looked glum.

A woman stood. "Yes, Mrs. Schloffski?" the Commander said and I recognized her from the *Sagan*.

"Ladies and gentlemen," she said dramatically, "I have been sorely distressed at the things said here tonight. Murder and insurrection have been advocated. I think it is time the saner, wiser heads in this Laboratory are heeded—goodness knows we have not been listened to enough in the past. In all honesty, I feel that if the Commander and his staff had sought out proper council among the Laboratory members we would not be having such difficulties now. I always thought—"

"Do you have a point, Mrs. Schloffski?" Commander Aarons said mildly.

"Of course I do. I wanted to say that, once the Council has spoken, we should be good enough citizens to recognize that fact and act accordingly. Certainly there is no one else to blame than ourselves for the fact that we have found so little of lasting scientific interest out here—"

"Who says?"

"How would *you* know?"

"—far from our natural home." She glared at the hecklers. "I believe there are a number of women who followed their husbands out from Earth and feel that they have sacrificed enough. The living conditions here are wretched. I imagine there will be many of us who will be *glad* to go home."

Mrs. Schloffski sat down. Her husband, sitting next to her, said something. She snapped at him and he opened his mouth and then closed it again. After that he was quiet.

"Commander?" my mother said, standing. "I would like to speak for the women *I* know. We are not ready to go Earthside until our jobs are finished here. We will stand by our husbands even if we don't have clean, ironed sheets every day."

There was a burst of applause. Several hands were waving for attention. The Commander picked my father's.

"Something bothers me about your wording, Commander. You said everyone returns on the *Argosy?*"

"Correct."

"I don't believe the Can's fusion plant and electrical generators can be left to automatic control; it's too risky. We will have to shut them down before we go."

"What's your point?" someone in the audience said.

"Without current our superconducting magnets will not work."

There was a murmur as a few people saw what Dad was driving at. Commander Aarons frowned and unconsciously tugged at his moustache.

"Without the magnets," my father went on, "the Can won't be completely shielded from the Van Allen belt radiation. High-energy electrons and protons will pass into the Laboratory. Within a year they will create enough radioactive isotopes to make the living quarters here uninhabitable. The isotopes will be distributed randomly around the Lab, in the walls and deck. The Lab will be unlivable."

The crowd was silent for a moment. An engineer said, "You mean men couldn't come back, ever? The Can would be contaminated?"

"It looks that way."

"Doctor Yakana is in charge of radiation control. Doctor, do you agree with Dr. Bohles?"

A lanky man near the front nodded.

"Those Earthside flea-brains!" someone shouted.

"Commander!" one of the ship's officers said. "Did the Council say they were abandoning the Lab?"

Aarons sighed. "My orders say 'The facility will be reactivated when fiscal policy permits.' That's all."

"When they speak in Latin it's always a brush-off," Zak said to me. The crowd was muttering, restless.

A ship's officer stood up. He was Lt. Sharma, a heavy, dark man from Calcutta who ranked middle-high on the squash roster.

"Sir, I think most of us have had enough of ISA," he said. "Right?" He turned to the audience and they answered with a storm of clapping.

"There's one thing the Council forgot. We don't have to cooperate! They can't force us. Who is going to send armed men all the way out to Jupiter?"

"I say we stay!" another voice said. "Refuse to board the *Argosy*. We'll thumb our noses at 'em."

Lt. Sharma shook his head. "Lord preserve me from my friends. That isn't what I meant. Not all of us can live out here indefinitely—we need trace elements in our diet, spare parts for the life system and a hundred other things."

"Okay, how long can we stick it out?" someone said.

"I am not qualified to say," Commander Aarons said. "You three—" he pointed out two bridge officers and the supervisor of Maintenance Division—"put your heads together and give us a guess."

The three women met in an aisle and murmured together for a moment while everybody watched. They nodded. "A little less than two years before we have serious trouble," one of them said.

"Thank you. I am no politician or economist, but I do not believe Earth's troubles will clear up in two years. The Council will not be able to send more ships by that time. And if we rebel now I *know* they're not going to be in the mood, anyway."

Lt. Sharma looked exasperated. "Sir, that is not what I had in mind."

"Oh?"

"Most of the Can's population must return Earthside. We'll never survive, otherwise. But we don't have to leave the project deserted. Leave behind a skeleton crew to keep the superconductors working, so that someday men can come back."

Mr. Moto stood up. "That sounds fine to me. We should leave a few scientists, too, to keep watch on Jupiter. Even simple, close-up observations covering the time the rest of us are gone will be immensely important."

"I volunteer," Mr. Jablons said.

"Me, too!"

"Single personnel should have preference."

"That's unfair!"

"Merde!"

"You can't—"

"Ich muss—"

"*Quiet!*" Commander Aarons tugged at his moustache. "All that will be decided later." He gazed slowly around the bowl. "I think we are all far too disturbed and hot under the collar to make reasonable judgments right now. I urge you all to think this matter through carefully; your lives may depend on it.

"I ask you then to go home and discuss it among your families. In a few days we will meet again. Good evening."

There was a burst of applause as he left the podium.

Jenny and Zak and I got out ahead of the crowd and headed for my home. People were pretty stunned. It wasn't until some time later that I remembered my date with Jenny; both of us had forgotten it.

"What do you think our chances are of staying on?" she asked me.

"Pretty grim. You can be sure any skeleton crew won't include us."

"Why has it got to be so few people?" Zak said. "We could cut out a lot of things, like the Ganymede base—"

"And have us climbing the walls and getting claustrophobic?" Jenny said. "No thankee."

"Well, we could stretch the lifetime of some of our machines by not using them so much. Take your shuttles; don't send them out so often. Save fuel, too."

"And if a satellite goes on the blink we just let it sit for a month?" Jenny said, tossing her head to arrange her hair. "What's the point of staying out here, if we can't get any research done?"

"I think we ought to abide by what the commander decides and not put up a squawk," I said. "Things will be touch and go when the *Argosy* arrives, as it is."

"What do you mean?" Jenny said.

"I'm not so sure the Council will expect us to come along meekly. They might have a few soldiers on that ship."

"Oh," she said.

"The bridge officers have firearms," Zak said.

"I know. And shooting off a hand weapon in a spaceship is stupid, but it might happen. One bad shot and everybody on that corridor will be breathing vacuum."

"You have a better idea?" Zak said.

"Sure," I grinned. "Hide. A few of us stay behind hidden—"

We were just crossing an intersection of two tubes.

"Typical," said a familiar voice. "But I didn't think you would admit it, Bohles."

Yuri came walking up. "Admit what?" I said.

"To being a coward," Yuri said. "Going to hide from the *Argosy* crew? Count on them not missing the skeleton crew that is left behind?"

"That was the idea," I said sullenly.

"You don't want to fight it out with them like a man, eh?" He gave me his confident smile. "No, you would rather hide the skeleton crew and act like a coward." He was playing this out for the benefit of Jenny and Zak. He casually folded his arms and smirked at me.

"Don't bother him, Yuri," Jenny said. There was a kind of plaintive note in her voice. As though she were pleading for me.

"No, *let* him bother me," I said, and hit Yuri in the mouth.

He looked surprised, then angry. The punch hadn't hurt him much. I blinked, and saw yellow sunlight, the school yard—

"You little—" he said, lowering his arms. I hit him again, harder. This time he stepped back, under the blow, and caught me solidly across the ribs. Suddenly I felt a cold tremor of naked fear.

That's where I lost track. I used fists, elbows and

even tried butting him with my head, and meanwhile Yuri was slamming his big ham hands into me, staggering me with every punch, making my eyes blur. I knew if I kept on and watched how his balance shifted just before he punched I could avoid most of the damage. And that meant I would win, because absolutely nothing was going to stop me from beating Yuri to a pulp, I told myself. *The dust, the jeering, bright sunlight.* . . .

Only . . . my arms were so heavy. . .

It took them forever to reach out and hit Yuri, and when they did I could feel the shock all the way to my shoulder. I was slowing down, and Yuri was speeding up. I felt the sharp pain of being hit—

Far away a voice said, "Hey! Break it up!" and a hand spun me around.

It was one of the bridge officers, frowning at me. I couldn't remember his name. My mind was a swirl of fear and self-disgust.

"If you two kids haven't got anything better to do than brawl, when the Lab is in deep trouble—"

"I'll take care of it, sir," Zak said, pulling at my sleeve. Yuri lowered his fists and snorted contemptuously at me. Jenny pushed him away. "Wo—won't happen again," I gasped.

Somehow the bridge officer disappeared and I was being led down a corridor, toward home. I stumbled blindly away.

The next morning I could hardly remember what had happened. Mom had patched me up, disinfected a cut over my cheekbone, and gave me a sedative. It must have been more than that; I went out like a light, and woke up with a dull buzzing in my head.

Neither Mom nor Dad mentioned the fight at breakfast. I didn't either; losers seldom do.

We did talk about the meeting, though. Dad came on rather pontifically about his obligation to his family and the fact that the Council might *never* send a relief expedition out to the Can's skeleton crew. It wasn't beyond ISA to drop the problem, political entanglements and all, and conveniently forget that there were men still circling Jupiter.

So, said Dad, the Bohles family would ship out on the *Argosy*. I pointed out to him that by the time the *Argosy* arrived I would be eighteen and technically a free adult.

That didn't go down very well. Dad frowned and Mom started to get tears in the corners of her eyes.

"After all," I said, feeling embarrassed, "you can't be *sure* ISA won't return. I'll come Earthside then."

Dad sighed. "No, it's not that."

"What is it, then?"

"You will be a stranger to us by then, Mattie," Mom said. "These next few years are the last ones we would ever have together as a family, and now . . ."

"Leyetta," Dad said. "Quiet. You can't shoulder the boy with that. He has to start finding his way alone now."

"Well, I didn't mean it quite that way," I said uncomfortably. "I don't want to break up the family. You're all I've got. But if I have a chance to stay here. . ."

"You should take it," Dad said decisively. "I would've done the same at your age."

"Paul!"

"It's true, Leyetta. A man has got to go his own way sometime."

"Don't worry, Mom." I searched around for some way to console her. "I probably won't be picked to stay, anyhow." But I knew very well that if I got the chance, I'd stick it out here.

"If you do stay, Matt," Dad said slowly, "be sure you come Earthside when you can. We don't want to lose track of you altogether."

"Huh? Why, you'll both be coming out as soon as ISA gets its head on straight."

Mom shook her head. "No, Mattie . . . In a few more years there will be others, just as capable *and* younger."

"No!"

"Yes, I'm afraid." Dad smiled slightly. "But let's not worry ourselves about that. Maybe there will be a way to weasel around the rules, who knows? The point that bothers me is that we came so close out here, we almost found life, and now it might be decades—hell, centuries!—before men get another crack at it."

"I don't see how you can be so sure there *is* life,

Paul," Mom said. "All I hear about is an endless series of negative results."

"Atmospheric Studies is going deeper and deeper with those bathyscaphes. If there is anything there—and there *must* be!—they will find it."

"Maybe they'll find something before the *Argosy* arrives," I said hopefully. "That would pull our chestnuts out of the fire."

"True." Dad sighed. "But some of our working time will be taken up with packing, shutting down the Lab, and compiling all the data we already have."

"Well, we can *try*."

"Of course. But don't expect miracles."

My mother said, "Paul do you think there's something to this idea of leaving some of us here to keep the Can alive? Honestly?"

"Ummmm. Well, maybe."

My mother curled one side of her mouth down, looking the way she sometimes does when she's thinking out a decision. "Well," she finally said, "in that case . . . I'm going to volunteer, too."

"*You*, Leyetta?"

"Mom, *why*?"

She looked steadily at us. "When I made that little speech last night, did you think I was talking like some kind of housewife? I must admit I sounded that way to myself. I was just trying to oppose that Mrs. Schloffski. But I came out here for reasons of my own, remember—not just to follow your father, Matt."

This was a facet of my mother I didn't know very well. "What do you mean, Mom?"

"Things are tight back on Earth, Matt. They have been for decades. That's why women haven't been getting jobs. The best work goes to men first. That's why there are women like Mrs. Schloffski. They hang on their men and get a lot of their identity out of what their husbands do. Mrs. Schloffski came out here to follow her family, not from any real interest in the Can. She's never really had anything better to do than housekeeping-type jobs, either on Earth or here in the Can. That's what makes her so, well, tedious."

"*I'll* say."

She smiled, her eyes distant. "I understand her fairly well, I think. That's what society can do to a woman. But some of us are lucky enough to have some work we're really interested in. *I* am. And that's why I'll stay, if I can."

Dad murmured softly. "Even if I can't?"

Her face crinkled. She was close to tears. "I don't know, Paul. I don't know."

I sat there and felt uncomfortable. These were layers in my parents I didn't know very well. The pressure and tension of these days was peeling them back, so I could see these inner parts for the first time. What my mother said applied to all the women in the Can, I supposed. Including Jenny. She hadn't said much about it, but Jenny wasn't the sort of female who would go back to a humdrum existence Earthside. Jenny had guts, just like my Mom. For Mom to even think of staying on while Dad shipped Earthside—well, that was a revelation. Sure, it wouldn't be forever, but still . . .

I sat there, mulling things over. Gradually, from the expressions on my parent's faces, I saw that it might be a good idea to leave them alone for a while. I jumped up and stammered out some reason to take off.

I went for a walk. Mom and Dad were trying to cover over their emotions some, but I could tell they were depressed. They liked life in the Can, despite the inconveniences—everybody did, except Mrs. Schloffski and other boneheads.

I passed by a work gang and looked for somebody I knew well enough to talk to. No luck. They were patching some resealant. I stopped for a moment and watched. Pressure imbalances and faults get a lot of attention. If you ever want to see people really move in the Can, holler "Vac alert!" I'd seen a kid do that once as a gag. He was on report for two years. I watched the women checking their work, and admired a slim calf or two. Everything was getting sort of jumbled up in my head these days—work and politics and sex (or the lack of it). I shook my head. Maybe all teenagers got as confused as I did, but I doubted it like hell.

I walked halfway around the hub and took an elevator inward to the Student Center. There was a big line of guys near the office. I prowled around and found Zak at the end of it.

"What's up?"

"They're taking names of men who want to stay behind."

"That's for me." I got in line. "Quite a few ahead of us."

"Guys have been waiting around all morning. I don't figure it matters when you sign up, though. They'll pick us by abilities."

"Seems reasonable."

"Okay for you, maybe. I'll probably wash out the first time the bridge officer reads the list."

"How come?"

"I ride herd on computers, and that's *all*. I can't pilot a shuttle, like you, and I don't know any electronics. I've spent all my time on math and learning how to tickle answers out of that overgrown abacus."

"Maybe you're right. If you've got a small staff, you might as well fill it with triple-threat men if you can."

"My reasoning exactly. I'm going through the motions anyway. Earthside will be bad, but I'll be better off than some of you guys."

"Why?"

"Remember that advertising slogan? 'You never outgrow your need for computers.' I can always get work somewhere, partake of the leisure of the theory class."

"Uh. I guess there won't be much to do for a shuttle pilot, now that space research is getting the axe."

"Next!" It was Zak's turn. He gave the standard information and was waved away. A bridge officer looked up at me with a sour expression.

"Matt Bohles," I said. "Any idea how many have signed up?"

"Too many. What's your job?"

"Shuttle pilot. I know some electronics, too—"

"Who doesn't?"

"—and I put in some time in Monitoring."

"Your father is in charge of Monitoring, isn't he?"

"Yes, but—"

The officer made a note. Maybe he figured Dad had just carried me on the rolls for a while. "How are you going to choose the men?" I said.

"We'll start with the ones who don't ask questions. Next!"

I wandered around with Zak. There were people everywhere; it felt like a festival day, only people were clumped together in knots, talking. We fooled around for a while and I mentioned my idea about hiding the skeleton crew instead of forcing the *Argosy*'s crew to leave them behind. Some of the other kids liked it; others said they preferred a fight, even if the Can's hull got punctured by accident. They seemed to be looking for a showdown and any handy enemy would do.

The talk wasn't getting anywhere—good grief, the *Argosy* was seven months away—so I dropped out and ambled down to Mr. Jablon's lab.

He wanted to talk politics, too. He'd thought of my idea, and found a hole in it big enough to drive a truck through: what if somebody like Mrs. Schloffski blabbed? That stumped me. We couldn't very well gag her, and the skeleton crew wouldn't tolerate leaving her behind. It looked like the only answer was a fight.

I swore off talking about politics; it made my head hurt.

"What I came down here for was some advice," I said, changing the subject. "I went out yesterday and found a crummy old Faraday cup on Satellite Fourteen. Can't we rig up something better?"

"Ummm," Mr. Jablons said. "What about that design you and I roughed out last year?"

"Well—" I hesitated. "The ones we built worked okay here in the lab, but they haven't been tried in space."

"We gave them two thousand hours of baking, bursts of radiation, the works. They came through."

"Right. They'll sure be better than the ancient one I saw."

"Which satellite?"

"Number Fourteen."

"Oh, that's it. Number Seventeen has the same type.

I've been nagging people to change those Faraday cups for years. Both Fourteen and Seventeen are in near-polar orbits. That makes them harder to reach by shuttle and thus far nobody's wanted to take the time just to replace a part that's working fine as it is."

"Well, I'll do it. Those old ones aren't sensitive enough for the job. Let's get the ones we designed out of storage."

It was a couple of hours before I got the new Faraday cups all checked out and packaged for carrying on the shuttle. They are delicate instruments and can't be thrown around like freight. It felt good to work with my hands and forget ISA, Yuri, the whole stinking mess.

I went up to the bridges to request a flight plan that intercepted Fourteen and Seventeen both; no use in making two trips. I could have requested the plan over intercom, but I wanted to stick a nose into the nerve center of the Can and sniff around.

The bridge is about two-thirds of the way out toward the rim, smack in the spot most thoroughly shielded from radiation by the mass of the rest of the Can. That's mostly to protect the magnetic memory elements in the computers; it also shortens lines of communication.

I got past one watch officer, but that was it. At the door to the bridge itself I was stopped and my request taken. I could see into the darkened volume beyond, where viewscreens shifted and threw up lines of incoming data faster than an untrained eye could read them. Commander Aarons was talking to some civilians—I couldn't tell who—and gesturing at a big display of an Earth-Jupiter orbit, probably the *Argosy*'s.

Then the officer cleared his throat, asked me if I had any more business, and suggested I move along. I shrugged and went to find Jenny.

It wasn't hard. She was standing in line to sign up for the skeleton crew.

"What's this?" I said.

"What does it look like?"

"Sheeg!" I said. "Every fish wants to be a whale."

"Any reason why a girl shouldn't be on the skeleton crew?"

"No, none really." Then I thought of something. "Do

you imagine the Commander will pick *two* shuttle pilots, though?"

"Of course not. Oh . . . I see what you mean. They'll split us up."

"If they take a shuttle pilot at all. Which I doubt. The skeleton crew is strictly a holding operation. No extras."

Her turn came just then. The bridge officer raised an eyebrow but said nothing; the military has never been a booster of equality for women.

When she was through I said, "Ready to do some work?"

"On what?"

I explained about the Faraday cups.

"Sure," she said. "Anything to get out of this madhouse."

I told my father over intercom that I would be gone until after midnight, ship's time, and to tell Mom not to wait supper on me; I would take enough suit rations. Dad hadn't heard anything new other than scuttlebutt. The latest rumor was that Commander Aarons had lodged a formal protest with ISA, without expecting it to do any good.

Dad mentioned that Monitoring had picked up more showers of rock orbiting into the Jovian poles; they seemed to be a regular occurrence now. The astronomers were busy trying to explain where they came from.

I told Jenny about the rumor on the way to the lock.

"Is *that* all he can do, lodge a formal protest?" she said. "Fat lot of good that is."

"All he can do until the *Argosy* arrives is talk. There will be plenty of time for action then. The Commander has already sacrificed enough for the Lab as it is."

"What do you mean?"

"Look, all the bridge officers are military men. When Lt. Sharma made that speech he was advocating that the Commander violate his orders—and Aarons accepted it. Even if he gets us Earthside and leaves a skeleton crew, he'll be cashiered. The bridge officers effectively ended their careers last night."

"Oh, I didn't realize that."

"We're civilians, we don't think in those terms. The Commander will never mention it, but it's a bald fact.

After we're Earthside we'll see a story in the fine print of a newsfax somewhere, and that will be it."

Jenny was quiet after that; I don't think she had realized quite what was going on.

We took the *Roadhog* again, with me in the pilot's chair. The orbit was already in *Roadhog*'s computer with a launch time about fifteen minutes later than we needed; I had asked the bridge for the margin, just in case I couldn't find Jenny right away.

Jupiter was a brownish, banded crescent, thinner than it was during our last flight. We boosted away from the Can on a long, elliptical orbit. Changing from equatorial to polar orbit costs fuel and time. We had to alter our velocity vector quite a bit to make rendezvous. Flight time was over six hours. I settled down to wait but I kept nervously checking meters and controls. I was jumpy.

"Hey, *sei still, Freund*," Jenny said. "*Was gibt?*"

"What gives? Oh, maybe I'm worried about meteoroids," I said, knowing I wasn't.

"I know what you mean," Jenny said, taking me seriously. "I found out from the bridge that Ishi was caught in one of those funny swarms we've been having."

"*What?* Why didn't they warn him?"

"The swarm was well clear of him, on radar. There must've been some small stuff that didn't show. It looked okay."

"How come they're letting us go out at all?"

"There's a lull, they say. No bunches of meteoroids coming in from the asteroid belt—"

"If that's where they're from. We don't know a frapping thing about them, or these storms, or what in hell is going to happen to us, to the Lab, to . . ."

"Hey, hey, easy," Jenny said softly, patting my gloved hand. "Just talk them out slowly. Don't let all your problems stack up on you."

So we talked. I told her about the mess with Yuri, about how I was angry and scared of him at the same time. I couldn't put it into words very well. My feelings were all mixed up inside. Compared to me Jenny seemed serene and sure of herself, and after talking to her I began to feel a little better, too. Between check-ins with the bridge, monitoring the storm activity, eating and getting some rest, we talked and mused about what was happening out here. The time passed quickly.

Satellite Seventeen was a glimmering white dot that swelled into a tarnished ball, even more decrepit than Satellite Fourteen. There were grainy patches where the polished metal skin had dulled and turned bluish-gold, for some reason. I snapped a few photographs for Mr. Jablons.

It took pretty long to install the new Faraday cups. The adhesive patch on my chest was crowded with components and I had to be sure I had all the microchips right.

Jenny left the *Roadhog* to help because it was impossible for me to hold everything in place and make high-vacuum welds at the same time. I couldn't even use magnetic clamps to hold all the parts in place, either, since the fields might disturb some of the instruments inside the satellite.

The bridge and Monitoring both confirmed proper functioning of the new Faraday cup; I thought I recognized Dad's voice.

Roadhog's ion engine boosted us over to intercept Satellite Fourteen, firing at maximum thrust all the way to make up time I had lost fiddling with Seventeen. I spotted it and tried to shave a little time off by doing the approach on manual. My distance perception was a little faulty; I overshot and had to backtrack with maneuvering jets.

Jenny handled a lot of the dog work on the installation this time. My reflexes were fouled up a little from simple muscle fatigue, but we got everything working well inside the bridge's allotted time. The window for our return orbit opened just as we were battening down. I gunned her hard enough to see a thin violet trail behind us, and we were on our way home.

Somebody once said that spaceflight is hours of boredom punctuated by seconds of terror. Well, there isn't much terror in shuttle work but there is plenty of boredom. Jenny and I slept most of the way back. The bridge woke me up once to report a steady rise in storm activity on Jupiter. I acknowledged, and thought I spotted more of those funny whirlpools before I fell asleep again. At the time I didn't much care if there was a three ring circus on Jupiter, complete with clowns; I was tired.

When I tucked *Roadhog* into her berth I topped off her fuel tanks and started running through a series of maintenance checks to be sure the instruments were still okay.

"Hey, don't you want to get inside?" Jenny said. She had just woken up and was grumpy.

"Sure," I said over the suit radio. "But I want to be sure *Roadhog* is ready to go out right away if I need her."

"Ummmm." She stretched. "We've been in her—what? —fourteen hours. Some time to suddenly become a stickler."

"Tourist!"

"Ummmm."

"A working cowboy waters his horse before he gets anything to drink himself."

"She's a horse now, is she? I thought she was a roadhog."

"Come on," I grinned at her through my faceplate. "I'll race you to the airlock. *And*—special today only, folks—I'll buy you that drink."

"Lead the way, my swain."

I woke up late the next morning with a funny ringing buzz in my head and eyes that didn't want to focus. Getting out of bed almost convinced me that the spin had been taken off the Can and my bedroom was now at zero-g—nothing moved quite right.

I recognized the symptoms. I had felt the same way when Dad introduced me to the black currant wine Mom brought down from Hydroponics; with no resistance or experience, it doesn't take very much to addle your brains.

Jenny and I hadn't really drunk a lot, but I guess it makes a difference *what* you drink, too. I'd experimented with hard liquor while she sipped an apertif wine. The evening had gone rather well: we sat in a corner of the darkened bar, meriting a few puzzled glances from the watch officers who came in after leaving duty. There was no one else around at those early morning hours, so our baptism into the rites of elders went unobserved by our friends, just the way we wanted it. We talked about the various illusions the sexes have, and how hard it is to see through them. It wasn't so much what was said, as how we said it. No resounding conclusions, but I learned a lot.

Then I had walked her home and kissed her good night. Now I had a hangover. How could life be more complete?

After a solid breakfast to get my blood sugar count up again, I felt pretty good. I resolved to learn a bit more about liquor before I tried some of the more exotic brands of rocket fuel the bar offered.

I got down to the Student Center during what would have been the normal morning coffee break, if these had been normal times. Kids are milling around the corridors trading rumors, with a particularly big clump at the bulletin board. I shouldered my way up near the front and saw a single typed notice:

PLEASE NOTE THAT IF, REPEAT, IF A SKELETON CREW IS LEFT BEHIND AT THE LABORATORY, *ONLY* SINGLE MEN OF MATURE YEARS WILL BE CONSIDERED.

COMMANDER AARONS

"Pooh!" a girl next to me said. "That boils it down to ship's officers."

"And some technicians," a boy said.

"And me," I put in.

"Didn't you read it all?" the girl said. "That 'of mature years' translates as 'no kids.' "

"Eighteen should be old enough," I said.

"Uh uh," the boy said. "That just means you're legally entitled to vote and carry a gun."

"What's a better definition of maturity?" I said sharply.

The guy shrugged. "Fight it out with Aarons if you want. I'm just giving you an educated guess."

"I need more than a guess."

I turned and worked my way out of the mob again. There weren't many kids in the Can in all, but they all seemed to be hanging around the Center. I wondered if any work was getting done, and then realized that it probably didn't matter to most of them; they had already mentally adjusted to the idea of shipping Earthside. It was a depressing revelation.

"Hey! Where are you going?"

"Oh, hi Zak." I stopped at the edge of the crowd. "I'm going to the bridge."

"Don't. I've already tried that gambit. Fifty other people thought of it first; the place is packed. They're not giving out any information, either."

"They've got to explain that notice."

"They haven't 'got' to do anything. The Commander probably wanted to stop people from pestering him with questions, so he eliminated most of them by ruling out women and married men. That's most of the Lab right there."

"What about us?"

"Who knows? Maybe they'll let eighteen-year-olds stay. Or maybe the Commander will stick with men who've been on the job a long time. I wouldn't be surprised if he kept it down to only officers."

"Why would he do that?"

"Figure it out. What have they got to lose? Earthside they'll be stripped of their commissions for disobeying orders. Why should they go back at all?"

"Well, I hope they don't fill all the slots."

"You really want to stay, don't you?" Zak said, looking at me oddly.

"Sure. Don't you?"

"Yes, but I'm not a fanatic about it. It's going to be pretty chancy staying in the Can without the *Argosy* and *Rambler* as backups."

"Think of all the material you would get for your diary. It would be an automatic bestseller."

"Huh! Boswell—the one who wrote *Life of Samuel Johnson*—used to feel that he hadn't really lived a day until he had written it up in his diary. I'm not *that* compulsive. There are better reasons to do things than just so you can put them in your diary."

"No more exciting chronicles of life among the supermen?"

"Not unless they pick me for the skeleton crew. Besides, there are some doubts buried deep in my poetic soul about the whole business."

"Huh?" I glanced at a wall clock. "Say, I want to get over to Monitoring to see my father. Come along for the walk, you probably need the exercise—"

"Health nut!"

"—and you can explain that last statement."

We went inward a few levels by elevator and started walking through a tangle of laboratories to reach Monitoring.

"Look," Zak said, spreading his hands, "call me a groundhog if you must, but it seems to me there's an ethical problem here. ISA is calling us back because Earth needs the money for social problems. Things are *tough* back there. People are eating sea yeast patties and living in each others' hip pockets."

"So are we."

"Voluntarily. Those people in India didn't raise their hands, they were born into it. What right do we or ISA or anybody have to take away money that might help them out?"

I walked along in silence for a moment. "I don't know. Maybe we haven't got a moral leg to stand on. But something tells me there's more to it. The same logic would have kept Columbus at home until all of Europe's slums were emptied."

"Right."

"How long would that be?"

"Uh? To clear the slums? Oh, I see. They're still there."

"And always will be. We keep upgrading the definition of 'slum.' Even so, I still don't think your argument stays afloat." I ambled along, hands stuck in my pockets, thinking. "I can't help but feel something basic will be lost if we give up ideas like the Jupiter Project. They're *dreams*—the things men live by."

"There will be other times in the future when we can come back out here."

"Yeah? When? A thousand years? There have been eras in Earth's history when men sat on their hands for that long, too poor or weak or scared to try something new. It could happen again, easy."

"Maybe so and maybe not. You don't *know* that would happen."

"There's the trick; you *never* know. Life is riding by the seat of your pants. We think new knowledge will pay off, sometime, but we aren't sure. All we know is that it always has before. Why should knowing about Jupiter be profitable? No answer. We don't know until we come. Is terraforming Ganymede a good idea? We won't know the answer to that one for a century or so, if then. Except if we *don't* do it where are we ever going to set up a self-supporting colony? The sociologists say small isolated communities are the best long term places for people. They keep people happy and productive. Ganymede might be a test of that in the long run—Earth hasn't fit that description in centuries.

"That's the whole trouble; the whole history of the human race has been one long unrepeatable experiment. Nobody's ever going to figure us out. So we might as well try everything we can, even if it hurts a little, to see what doors it opens up."

"Lecture over?"

"Yeah. Sorry."

"That's okay. I have a funny feeling you're right. It *feels* right, anyway. Something has got to be wrong with a system that says Michelangelo shouldn't have taken money to do the Sistine Chapel as long as everybody wasn't eating prime beef."

I nodded. The walls of the corridor were painted in a red spiral to give the feeling of depth, but at the moment the effect just made me a little dizzy. We came to Monitoring and Zak waved good-bye. I went in.

Dad looked up from his notes. Mr. Jablons was with him.

"Come on in son. You're just in time to see if your Faraday cup design holds up."

Chapter 13

There was a third man I vaguely recognized, wearing African robes.

"Matt, this is Dr. Kadin. He is the Laboratory Science Director." Dr. Kadin bowed slightly and smiled. I remembered that he was Dad's boss; in fact, he was the head of all the scientific research done in the Can and on Ganymede. I made the appropriate introductory noises while I tried to figure out why he was here.

"There are large storms brewing at Jupiter's poles," Dr. Kadin said to me. "Over the last few weeks I have been working with the astrophysicists to find an explanation. We have had little success. We do, however, think the storms may be throwing great swarms of electrons and other particles completely out of the Jovian atmosphere. Once above the ammonia cloud layer, they may become caught in Jupiter's magnetic fields and funneled into the Van Allen belts. It is, of course, only a hypothesis." He smiled again, showing incredibly white teeth.

"It's a good thing you installed those new cups," Mr. Jablons put in. "They'll give us much better resolution of the electron concentration around Satellites Seventeen and Fourteen."

"Because Seventeen and Fourteen pass close over the poles?" I said.

"Correct," Dr. Kadin said precisely. "If your design can function under high particle flux, we may be able to record some highly significant data. There are some theoretical reasons to believe these particles originated deep in the Jovian atmosphere, perhaps deeper than we have ever been able to probe before."

"When does it happen?" I said.

Dad glanced at a clock. "About now. I've been trying to reach you at home and down at the Student Center, with no luck. Thought you might want to watch. Satellite Seventeen should enter the polar region any moment."

Dad thumbed the panel on his desk and his viewscreen began registering a readout from the Hole. The watch officer had set up a simple moving graph to show the particle flux that Satellite Seventeen was registering. The black line had already started a gradual climb. We all crowded around the screen, just about filling Dad's office.

"That is an expected result," Dr. Kadin said after a moment. He poked a finger at the rising line. "We can correlate this data with information from other equatorial satellites, to find the energy and other characteristics of the particles. The important point is how high this line can go."

Mr. Jablons shuffled nervously. We waited, watching the line climb faster and faster. The only sound was a background whirr of air circulation.

The line rose, rose—and then dropped. It fell straight down to zero.

Dr. Kadin frowned, "It should not do that."

We waited.

My face began to feel hot.

The line didn't move.

"The Faraday cup may have shorted out," Mr. Jablons said finally.

"Yes. It would seem so." Dr. Kadin glanced at me, then looked quickly away. "Unfortunate."

My father cleared his throat. "If the instrument has failed there is nothing to be done."

"But it *couldn't* fail!" I said.

"Quiet, son. Remember, Dr. Kadin, Satellite Fourteen crosses the same region above the pole in—" a look at the display screen—"three hours. We can get some data then,"

"Yes. Good." He looked at me, not smiling. "The old Faraday cup would have given at least some information throughout the satellite's passage over the pole. Hmmmm. Well—I shall return in three hours."

With that he swept from the office, red robes fluttering.

Dad and Mr. Jablons tried to cheer me up but I wasn't having any. We all knew that design worked. I must have installed it wrong. Maybe the job on Fourteen, with Jenny helping, was okay. Maybe.

One thing was clear: the radiation level in the Van Allen belts was rising fast. Dad made a note to advise the bridge and recommend that no men or craft be allowed outside the Can for the duration of the storm. I fooled around in the Hole, keeping tabs on Satellite Fourteen while it orbited up from the equator toward Jupiter's north pole, toward the splotchy indigo storms.

After a while I took a break and wandered down to the Center. I was feeling pretty rotten. I ran into Jenny and she told me about a square dance that evening. That cheered me up; it would take my mind off everything that was going wrong with my life. Normally I dance as if someone was firing pistols at my feet, but with Jenny . . .

That's when I got an idea. I looked around for an intercom phone and asked Jenny to wait a minute.

"Bridge," a flat voice answered.

"This is Bohles. I'd like a provisional trajectory computed for rendezvous of shuttle *Roadhog* with Satellite Fourteen. Departure in, umm, two hours fifty minutes from now."

"Well, okay, but we're expected to close down external operations any minute now. Background count is too high."

"Transmit it to *Roadhog*'s computer anyway, will you? I can clear the computer tomorrow if the program is invalidated."

"Okay, if you just want to make work for yourself. I'll beam it over in a couple of minutes."

"Right, thanks."

I hung up and went back to Jenny.

"What's up?"

"Oh, nothing," I said. "Had lunch yet?" I kept my voice cool and casual. Inside I was tense, calculating, making plans.

"Yes, I ate earlier . . ." Jenny peered at me, looking puzzled. I avoided her eyes.

"Oh, okay, I . . . I think I'll go get something." I waved good-bye and moved off.

I got a snack. Then I went for a walk, alone. I didn't

really want to talk to Jenny, or anybody else. Things were boiling up in me, things I couldn't explain.

I watched the faces in the curving corridors. Tight faces, sad ones. Frowns. Scowls. Distracted looks. Dazed expressions. People who seemed like they'd just come from a really terrible argument. Usually you see smiles. But now . . .

The spirit we once had was seeping away. I could feel it. We'd all been special out here. A pocket of light and air, bathed in hard radiation and unbearable cold. An outpost.

But now . . . They all knew we were going back. Crawling back home, defeated by the mysteries of Jupiter and the blindness of Earth . . .

Ignorant bastards, I thought moodily. People passing by glanced at me. I realized I must have said it out loud.

I leaned against a bulkhead, feeling suddenly dizzy. Christ, what was happening to me? I was wandering at random, talking to myself.

Things were moving too fast. Problems were coming up and nobody was solving them. Dr. Matonin went around with her oh-so-concerned smile, but that did no good. And Commander Aarons had already written off any chance of a kid staying here. The plain truth of the matter was that, to them, kids were just kids. In a tight situation, it was the adults who counted. Adults knew best. Kids only *thought* they had problems . . . try to tell an adult what was really eating at you, and you'd get the old chuckle and a nod of the head, and then a piece of warmed-over advice. They didn't really see us as equals, as people, at all . . .

I marched through the decks, muttering to myself, hands clenching and unclenching.

Dr. Kadin arrived a few minutes after I got back to Monitoring. I studied the reports from equatorial satellites. The radiation being fed into the belts had dropped in the last hour, almost down to the permissible level for shuttlecraft operation.

"Do you suppose the storm is dying out?" I asked Dad. He peered at his viewscreen, which at the moment was focused on a gigantic orange whirlpool in the ammonia clouds. "There isn't any way to tell. The storm activity seems to be related to the number of vortex formations in the atmosphere, and there aren't any new ones building up right now."

"There may be a relatively quiet time coming up," Dr. Kadin put in, "much like the eye of a hurricane. I must say this is all very queer and extraordinary. There has been nothing like it in the nine years we've been here. I hope Satellite Fourteen will give us the data we need."

"Where is Fourteen?" Mr. Jablons asked.

Dad switched to another input and reported, "Two minutes until anything significant could register."

Dr. Kadin got a distant look in his eye. "You know," he said, "so many curious things are happening at once, it is enough to make one wonder. We have recorded massive thunderstorm activity deep in the atmosphere. Great bolts of lightning."

"The formation of living cells requires lightning, doesn't it?" I asked. "Electricity can energize the manufacture of molecules—like the ones we know are down there in the clouds—to produce living compounds."

"So experiments on Earth have shown," Dr. Kadin agreed, raising his eyebrows and sighing. "But we have never found such things in Jupiter. Perhaps lightning is not all that is needed."

"What about those meteor swarms?" Mr. Jablons put in. "What's the explanation for them?"

"I am afraid today is not a bright one for the scientists. Our expert on the asteroid belt says they may come from there. Another says the orbits trace back to Jupiter's own moon system. There remain many questions; we do not have sufficient data. The odd thing is that the swarms strike Jupiter near the poles, not the equator. Very unusual—"

"The Faraday cup on Satellite Fourteen is beginning to register an increase," Dad said.

We all crowded around his desk. Dr. Kadin fidgeted at his robes. Mr. Jablons tapped a pencil on his knee. Distant murmurs from the Can underlined the silence between us.

The black line rose again. I clenched my fists, watching it, not daring to move. The only sound was the pinging of a recorder.

"Looks good," Mr. Jablons said hopefully.

Dr. Kadin said nothing.

The line shot up, climbing to nearly the same level Seventeen had registered. It held there, steady, steady, holding—

And fell.

In a moment, the readings dropped to zero. The Faraday cup wasn't working.

"Well," Dr. Kadin said. "I had hoped—"

I couldn't listen to it. I turned and bolted from the room.

"Matt!" my father called after me. I didn't look back.

I ran down the corridor, blinking back tears of anger. That cup *couldn't* fail, I just knew it!

I took an express elevator inward, toward the center of the Can. The tube that led to the air lock was deserted. Nobody was going outside now, during the storm.

I forced myself to calm down a little once I was in the suiting-up bay. It wouldn't be smart to foul up an air hose and find out about it in the middle of decompression.

I left the bay, carrying my helmet under my arm, and stepped into the short passageway that led to the main air lock. It would be a good idea to cycle the lock manually; the bridge might notice it on their board if I put the lock on automatic. I put a hand on the hatch wheel.

"Hey, shrimp, what're you doing?"

I didn't say anything. I turned the wheel faster. I heard Yuri's steps behind me.

A hand landed on my shoulder and spun me around.

"There's a storm, kid. Nobody goes outside."

"I've got permission."

"Oh? From who?"

"Commander Aarons. Ask him."

"A likely story."

"It's true. Go on, ask him. He's right over there." I pointed down the corridor.

Yuri turned his head, following my finger. My heart was beating furiously. The cold fear began to seep into me again and I hesitated. I knew this was it. I would get only one chance.

Yuri frowned in disgust and started to turn back toward me.

I slammed my fist into his stomach.

"Hey!" He staggered back.

I jabbed at his chin. Yuri blocked and hit me in the shoulder. I backed off. He came crowding in on me, fast. I swung and missed. Yuri brushed my arm aside, and landed a solid punch in my stomach, knocking the wind out of me.

The world turned purple. I jabbed and caught him weakly on the chest. Something slammed into my face. I reeled back, gasping. He hit me twice more and I went down.

"Dumb, really dumb." He prodded me with a toe.

I lay face down on the polished deck. *The dust, the goddamned yellow dust. The crowd heckling, laughing. Coward, weakling . . . the spattering sound . . .*

I was down, but I wasn't really badly hurt.

I blinked and the drifting purple mist faded away. I breathed deeply.

And I reached inside myself, deep, into the cold ball of fear at the center of me. I saw it for what it was. And I smothered it, pushed it away.

I forced myself up onto my hands and knees.

Yuri smirked at me. "Come on, I think I will take you to see the officer of the watch. He should be most interested in—"

I brought my thigh up and shot my leg out in a frontal kick, the way I'd seen it done on 3D. Yuri started to turn. The kick caught him in the side. He staggered, off balance, "Wha—"

I leaped at him. I gave him two quick jabs in the side of the head. He whirled and hit me in the stomach. Pain lanced through me. I gritted my teeth and stood my ground. I landed three punches on his chest. Yuri slowed. I slammed my fists into him again and again and again and suddenly he wasn't there anymore.

I looked down. He was lying on the deck. He didn't move but he was breathing. I didn't think he was hurt. At the moment I didn't care much one way or the other. Yuri had been dishing out a lot of crap lately. I figured he could take his chances.

I left him there. Sure, I could tie him up, but what if somebody else came along while I was doing it?

I cycled out of the lock, breaking the hatch open before the red light winked green. A burst of air blew me away from the lock, tumbling. I sucked in a sour breath of suit air. *Time, time. . . .*

I leveled off using attitude jets and picked out the *Roadhog*'s berth. I cruised over to it. I felt lightheaded; I automatically checked my oxygen level to see if I was hyperventilating. The meter didn't say so; the effect was probably from adrenaline. I could hear my pulse tripping in my ears.

I coasted into the seat after clearing the mooring lines. I backed *Roadhog* out of her berth in one burst. I set a beeline course for the mouth of the Can and thumbed on the autopilot. Good; the course for Satellite Fourteen was logged in. Departure time in five minutes. Well, that would have to be close enough; I couldn't hang around waiting, and *Roadhog* would clear the Can in less than two.

I ran a quick check on the shuttle. One of the forward lines had vapor-locked, but I overloaded the pressure and blew it open. It would probably be okay for the trip, I told myself.

We passed pretty close to the *Sagan* going out. It was eerie, being alone in the bay. There were no work lamps, no other moving craft, only the pinwheeling lights of the Can.

We had just cleared the Can. I slammed on the drive. The boost pushed me back in my seat with a gratifying weight. We went hell for leather out the top, burning fuel extravagantly. I wanted to get away, and fast. I'd use up some of my safety reserve, but it was worth it. Ten minutes out, I switched in the computer orbit. *Roadhog* stirred under me. She pointed her nose at the glowing crescent of Jupiter and I felt the ion engine kick in on a new vector. We were off.

Roadhog ran steadily for a few minutes before the radio came alive.

"Bohles! This is the bridge. We have just picked you up on radar. Turn around. Radiation levels—"

I switched it off. After I had given the *Roadhog* a thorough check I clicked it back on again.

"—mander Aarons speaking. I order you to return to the Laboratory. You can accomplish nothing this way."

"I don't think he's listening, sir. We haven't had a peep out of him."

"Hmmmm. Can someone go out and get him?"

"Not too easily. Those shuttles have big engines on them for their weight. He's already moving pretty fast."

"How long to pick him up?"

"Two hours, minimum."

"Not good enough. I can't ask someone to risk his life—"

"Don't bother," I said. "I'll take all the risks."

There was a pause. Then: "Bohles, this is a very foolish thing to do. There is no need—"

"Listen, I'd like to talk to my father."

Faintly: "Where's his father? On intercom? Patch him in."

"Hello, Matt?"

"Hi, Dad." My voice seemed thin, weak. I swallowed. "This isn't very smart."

"I've got to *do* something. I don't want to go Earthside, Dad. You said yourself that we've got to justify keeping the Lab out here by solid results. Well, maybe it's too late, but I'm going to try."

"Son . . ."

"What is the radiation level along my orbit?"

A pause. "Well, you are a little lucky there. The background count seems to be falling off. Maybe there is going to be a lull in the storm, but you are taking a chance."

"Anybody who keeps breathing takes a chance."

"Matt, your mother would like—"

"No, no." I didn't think I could take that. "Don't put her on."

In the background: "If the pattern holds, sir, the radiation levels will be acceptable." "Hmmmm. Cancel that order to intercept." "I think he has a good chance to come out of it all right, sir." "But you don't know, do you?" "Uh, nossir."

"Dad?"

"Yes, Matt. Your mother—"

"No. I'm signing off. I'll let you know if anything changes. I'm not eager to get a radiation burn out here, either. But I believe this is worth the risk."

"I think Yuri will be around to look you up when you get back, too." I could imagine him smiling as he said it.

"Tell him I'll be receiving visitors. And don't worry. I'll be okay. I want to think things over out here. Alone."

"I hope—"

"Good-bye." I switched off.

Loneliness is a sad word; solitude is more dignified. But loneliness is just solitude you don't want, and there were times in the hours ahead when I would have given anything if Jenny or Zak or anyone had been there.

For a while I watched the radiation gauge every two minutes. It dropped a little but not much. My radio emergency light blinked a few times; I ignored it.

The journey became almost hypnotic. Jupiter was a thin crescent sliced by the familiar bands. I could make out some of the outer moons; Ganymede was a faint blue disc. Io trailed behind me, an orange-red ball that fell below as I moved toward Jupiter's north pole. Satellite Fourteen was coming down to meet me.

I watched the huge whirlpools catch up and pass below me. At their centers I could see dark blotches— methane? frozen water?—swirling in a grand, lazy dance. It was hard to believe those blemishes were larger than the Pacific Ocean.

Jupiter filled the sky. This close it is more like an infinite plain than a planet and you can't really be convinced that you aren't going to fall into it. Beyond the terminator, in what should have been blackness, I could see thin fingers of yellow lightning playing in cloud banks.

Perhaps Jupiter was the home of the gods and the storms were merely giant tournaments; Jove throwing his thunderbolts . . .

I caught myself right there. Men have been hypnotized by Jupiter's vastness before me and I recognized the symptoms.

I gave myself some rations, savored them to stretch out the time, and busied myself by climbing around the *Roadhog* and looking her over. The superconductor fields were working okay. Because of them I couldn't climb over the side and inspect the undercarriage. I called the Can a few times. After a few tries at persuading me to come back, the bridge officer gave me radiation level readings. They matched pretty closely to mine.

I didn't think very much about the radiation. I was getting a little more than the "acceptable" dose, but that was just an average worked out for people in all sorts of jobs. If I got a lot there were treatments that would help.

Even if I didn't make it—so what? Nobody lived forever. I wouldn't live to see the first star ship leave; I'd never know if there were intelligent life forms living near the Centauri system, or Tau Ceti, or . . .

I caught myself again. No use getting morbid.

Minutes crawled by, then hours. I dozed.

My radio emergency light was blinking an angry red when I woke up. I ignored it and checked the time. Rendezvous should be coming up.

I looked around to orient myself. Jupiter was still a striped custard below; now I could see a purple darkening toward the pole.

In a few minutes I picked out a white dot that seemed a likely candidate. It grew. I matched velocity and watched Satellite Fourteen resolve itself into an overweight basketball.

I coasted over. The Faraday cup didn't show any damage; everything looked just the way I had left it.

I disconnected it from the satellite's electrical system and checked carefully over the outside. Nothing wrong. The heart of a Faraday cup is the grid trapping mechanism. I would have to open it up to get a look at that.

I unclipped a no-torque screwdriver from my suit belt and took the cover off the cup. Everything still looked okay. I removed the backup shields and slid the center of the cup out. It was just big enough to hold in one hand.

The final cover came off easily. Then I saw what was wrong.

The space between anode and cathode was filled with some sort of oil.

I thought back. Oil? That didn't make sense. I was sure it wasn't there when I installed the cup. It wasn't oil, anyway. It was more like sticky dust. I poked a finger into the gap. Some of the stuff stayed on my glove; some more drifted away into space.

I swore. An electrical failure I could understand, but this was out of my department.

What about that old Faraday cup I'd replaced? I hadn't even looked at it. I'd just let it drift away from the satellite, since I didn't have any further use for it. Maybe that one had this gunk in it, too.

One thing was certain: I wasn't going to fix it out here. I took out a plastic sheet and wrapped up the part, dust and all.

I got back in the *Roadhog*, waved good-bye to Fourteen and fired the ion engine.

The work had made me hungry again. I ate some rations and then finally answered my radio.

"Matt?" It was Mr. Jablons.

"Who else?"

"I thought you might like to know that Satellite Seventeen's cup cleared up a while ago. There appears to be some saturation phenomenon operating."

"Oh, great. You mean if I'd left the cup on Fourteen alone it would fix itself?"

"Probably. Are you bringing it in?"

"Yes."

"We'll need a look at it anyway. A device that fails only when you need it isn't much use. I'll meet you at the lock and get right on the problem."

"Fine."

After some chatter about the radiation, which was rising again, I switched over to the bridge. They estimated that if the storm followed the same pattern as it had earlier, I wouldn't get too much of a dosage.

It was a race to get me back to the Can as soon as possible. I was in the fastest possible orbit right now, so there wasn't much to be done.

"Connect me with Zak Palonski, would you?" I said. While I waited, my headphones beeping and clicking, I reviewed what I'd been thinking about the last few hours. This wasn't going to be easy to say.

"Matt? Boy, when you go overboard you do it in a big way."

I grimaced. "Yeah. I—I went *crazy* back there, Zak. Once I got away from the Can and cooled off, I could see that. And why. It's related to something you told me, once."

"You mean about that fight back when you were a kid? And Yuri?"

"Right. I've gotten them all scrambled up, Zak. That eight-year-old Matt Bohles got so damned scared he was frantically *glad* to get away from Earth. I mean, I must've identified those bullies with the way *all* Earthside was going to be. I cried every night for weeks after that fight, you know."

"So the little kid thought all the rest of life was going to be getting pushed around, bullied."

"Yeah." I smiled to myself, thinking back. "Yeah, I can still remember some of those feelings, now that I understand. When we got out to the Can it was—wow! —like being reborn. Everybody was nice. The bigger kids didn't gang up on me."

"You could be the smart guy without getting punished for showing off. You didn't have to be a phony tough guy."

"Yeah—say! How come you know all that?"

"Hell, you think you're so different? We're all kids from pretty highbrow families. We all had those fears."

"Then why—?" I sputtered.

"I noticed some funny symptoms when Yuri started hassling you. I mean, I figured we kids were all over that stuff by now—but you didn't seem to be. The way I see it, something about Yuri—his size, maybe—made you regress, go back to the behavior pattern you had in that Earthside playground. You couldn't deal with him. You retreated into—"

"Dammit! Why didn't you tell me? I—"

"I didn't *know*. It was just a hunch. Young Freud, remember? I had to give you a chance to work it out yourself, even though I could see something was bothering you, and it was getting worse. Just telling you wouldn't have worked either. You had to come on it yourself or it wouldn't ring true. Remember when you had that dream on Ganymede and I started in on you?"

"Zak the head-shrinker, yeah."

"You brushed me off."

"Yeah," I said quietly.

We were silent for a moment. I could hear Zak breathing into his mike. "Hey, look," he said awkwardly. "What was it some philosopher said?—'Self knowledge is usually bad news.' But that's not necessarily so."

I nodded. "Right. Right. Now that I see it, I think I can deal with it. I'm *scared* of going Earthside. I like it out here. It's *safe*." I laughed recklessly. "No schoolyards for the big kids to beat me up in."

"I figure you'll make it, Matt." Zak said warmly. "I really do."

"I'd better." My sudden elation fizzled out. "Aarons will ship me Earthside for sure."

"Huh? Why?"

"I went berserk, Zak. Crazy. Unstable. I swiped this shuttle, risked my life, broke regs, beat up Yuri . . . God, that felt good . . ."

"I see your point," Zak said sadly. "*I* know you'll be okay now, but Aarons doesn't have any choice."

"Yeah," I said. I looked down at Jupiter, endlessly spinning, and felt a bone-deep weariness. "I'm washed up, Zak. This time I'm really finished."

"Matt?"

"Huh?" I felt drowsy. "Yes?"

"We've got trouble." It was Dad.

"I'm only thirty-three minutes from ETA. What could—"

"That's the point. We've just picked up a big flare on the south pole. Some extraordinary activity."

"Meaning—?"

"Looks like a burst of high energy stuff, headed out along the magnetic field lines. The whole Jovian magnetosphere is alive with radio noise. And higher than the normal radiation flux, of course."

"Will it catch me?"

"Looks like it."

"Damn." I bit my lip.

"Your fuel is—"

"I've already checked. Just enough to brake, maybe a fraction over."

"I see." A silence.

I frowned, calculating. I gave the idea about five seconds of solid thought, and then I knew: "Give me a new orbit, Dad. I'm firing along my present trajectory, as of—" I punched the stud—"now."

A solid kick in the small of my back.

"Wait, Matt, we haven't computed—"

"Doesn't matter. Sooner I get going, the more seconds I'll shave off my arrival time."

"Well . . . yes," Dad said slowly.

I held my thumb on the button, eyeing my fuel tank. Burn, baby. Go! But not too much—

I raised my thumb. The pressure at my back abruptly lifted. "What's my mid-course correction?" I barked.

"We—we plot you into a delta-vee of zero point three seven at five minutes, forty-three seconds from now." Dad's voice was clipped and official. "Transmitting to your inboard on the signal."

I heard the *beep* a second later. I was on my way. The new course correction would bring me into the Can with minimum time.

"How much did I pick up?"

"I make it seven, no seven point four minutes."

"That enough?"

"It's close. Damned close."

"Better than frying."

"Yes, but. . . ."

"Yeah, I know. What's my reserve?"

"None."

"What?"

"None. It will take about every gram of fuel to get you to the top of the Can, instead of flying by at several klicks farther out. You may have a few seconds of juice left at the bottom of the tank, but it can't be more than a small fraction of what you need."

"Geez."

"Son, you'll come into the top pancake."

"With no brakes."

"Right."

"Damned magnetosphere. What's *causing* all this, Dad? I mean—" I pounded my gloves on the steering column— "why in the *hell* does the solar flux have to stack up on us just when Jupiter is throwing out this crap? What's happening at the poles?"

"I don't know. We've never seen—"

"I *know* that. But, but—" Then I shut up. I was just whining, and I knew it. The universe plays for keeps. It doesn't give a damn if you're a screwed-up kid who has gone off on a dumb stunt. Whining wouldn't help.

The minutes crawled by. I made the course correction and watched the Can grow from a bright dot into a slowly spinning target. I fidgeted. I planned. I talked to Dad, but there wasn't much to say.

I had somewhere between zero and maybe ten seconds of burn time left. Not enough to slow me down much.

I climbed over the rig, detaching every unit and pouch and box that I could shove overboard. The less mass I had, the more braking I could get out of those few seconds of impulse.

I took the Faraday cup and put it in my carrybag, tucked on the inside of my left leg so nothing could easily bump it. They're mechanically pretty strong, anyway.

Then I looked at the stars for a moment, trying to think. I had to stay calm and I would have to move fast. I kept thinking that there had to be some way out of this.

The bridge was sending a team out to help. There wasn't much they could do, of course. There wasn't much time to deploy a shuttle and boost it out to meet me, match velocities and make a pickup.

The Can arced across from my left, swelling. I swung my scope forward. I could make out the pancake. I was coming in almost edge-on. Were those specks moving? Maybe they were the team that was waiting for me. Or maybe just my imagination.

"Thirty seconds." Dad's voice was stiff, tight.

The silvery skin of the Can looked like a Christmas

tree ornament. Funny, how I'd never noticed that before. The big cylinder grew and grew against the flat black of space. Stars beamed silently at me. The pancake was spinning serenely, faster than the Can. It was just a big bag of water, but at these speeds—

I saw the idea at the last possible moment. If I ran into the right side of the pancake, its spin angular momentum would be directed against me. But on the *left* side, the spin would be *with* me. The relative velocity between *Roadhog* and the pancake would be less. So if I could—

I spun the attitude jets to the right. The pancake was growing, dead ahead. How much should I give it?

Too much and I'd miss entirely. Miss, and shoot past the Can. And the radiation would fry me. When they finally fetched me back home and cracked my suit, I'd look like a potato chip.

But if I gave it too little, the shock of impact would shatter *Roadhog* and me along with it.

I fired the jets. One second, two, three—

I cut it off. We glided leftward. The pancake was a huge spinning sack of water, and I was flying toward it and now laterally across it, closing fast—

—too fast—

I saw specks of light. People. Waving. The pancake became a vast spinning plain. I came shooting toward the edge of it. I could see the thick organiform skin sliding away below me, moving the same direction as *Roadhog*, but slower. We were vectoring down into the plane, like a needle falling toward a spinning record—

There was shouting in my suit phones. I ignored it. I had been so worried about hitting the pancake, but now I *wanted* to hit it, wanted it so bad I could taste it.

I had the engine into braking mode already. But when should I fire? Distances were hard to judge. I could see stenciling on the pancake's skin now, numbers shooting by below. Closer. Closer—

I jammed a thumb down on the firing stud. One, two . . . five seconds. The silvery wall of the pancake edge rose up before me, blotting out the stars, Seven—Eight— Dead. The engine gurgled to a stop.

The pancake was turning, sliding away. But I was catching up with it. And suddenly I saw that the physics wasn't as simple as I thought. Once I hit the organiform, what would keep me there? There was no gravity. I would rebound from the pancake and go tumbling off into—

But I could use the friction of the grainy organiform. And maybe grab a handhold. Maybe—

My adhesive patch. It would help hold me to the rough surface. I reached up toward my neck and yanked down. Then I slapped my knee with the tab and—

We hit.

The forward strut caught the pancake skin. It dug in.

I ducked my head and wrapped my arms over my neck. Standard position. A shock ran through *Roadhog*. I felt a grinding tremor—

A pipe smacked me in the ribs. I slammed into something that gave slightly. All around me bright, glittering debris was tumbling, like a luminous shower. Sparkling bits of *Roadhog* plunged by me. Soundless. Soundless, and tumbling.

I rolled over and over, along the face of the pancake. My adhesive patch caught, gave way, caught, gave way, making a small ripping sound inside my suit. It kept me on the pancake, reduced the recoil momentum, but it wasn't slowing me down much.

I snatched at a handhold. Caught it. Lost the grip. The organiform is rough, but flexible. I rolled, arms curled over my head, legs out straight. A waterfall of junk was tumbling with me. My right side and arm hurt, but there was no jabbing pain. Maybe the organiform had cushioned me enough; maybe nothing was broken.

The adhesive patch was snatching at the organiform, holding me to it. But I wasn't stopping. I was rolling in a soundless shower. Outside my helmet was a blur of gray organiform, then a blur of black sweeping by, then organiform again. If it went on I would roll off the top of the pancake and out into space.

I brought my arms down, dug in with my elbows. At once I got a jarring and my arm twisted painfully. I tried again. Another wrenching jolt, a flash of pain in my shoulder.

If I wasn't careful, I'd push too much against the

pancake and knock myself off entirely, out into space. I
fought against the sickening revolution and tried to scan
the pancake skin ahead. I was near the edge. Friction with
the pancake was trying to swing me around, give me some
angular deflection. But ahead of me I could see pieces of
Roadhog flying off into the blackness.

Ahead, something—A blur. No, a bump. A set of
handholds in the plastiform.

It came looming up. I thrashed toward it. The white
bumps shot toward me. I kicked in their direction without
thinking. I began to rise off the pancake. I was rebounding
off. I snatched—Missed. Another handhold came gliding
by below. I windmilled my arms, bringing my head
toward the pancake. I snatched downward. Grabbed it.
Held on for the jolt—

When my arms felt like a bundle of knots, I knew I
had it. I flailed wildly and got my other hand onto it. My
arm was numb. I dumbly watched pieces of *Roadhog*
disappear over the side, spinning away into the darkness.

"Matt! You okay?"

"I . . . I think so."

"Don't waste time! Get over to the lock!"

"Yeah . . . sure . . . Maybe the team can . . ."

"It's faster if you follow the emergency line to the
ten-A lock."

"Oh . . . okay."

I started hand over fist along the skin of the pancake,
working my way toward the bright blue emergency line
twenty meters away.

Inside Lock ten-A I sagged against the bulkhead and
listened to the hiss of air flooding in around me. I looked
down. My adhesive patch looked like somebody had been
trying to snatch it bald. There were cuts and nicks all over
my suit. I still had the goddam Faraday cup sealed in the
carry-bag on my left leg. My leg ached there; it must have
banged against me. But through the clear plastic the cup
didn't look damaged. I thought, *Well, that's what this was
about, right?* It looked like pretty small stuff.

I waited for the lock to cycle. I was wrung out,

depressed. I half expected to be met by the ship's officer who would put me in handcuffs.

But then the lock swung open. The tube outside looked like a subway car. People were jammed in. They waved and beamed as I stepped forward. I popped my helmet and a warm rush of noise poured in.

"Matt!" My mother wrapped her arms around me and cried.

Dad was there, smiling and frowning at the same time, shaking hands with me.

People were swarming around, touching me, helping me off with my suit.

Mr. Jablons appeared at my elbow. "Welcome back." He took the Faraday cup in its wrapper. "Good luck with the boss, too." His eyes twinkled and he gestured with his head at Commander Aarons, who was talking to an officer down the corridor.

"How do you feel, Matt?" I turned the other way and saw Jenny.

"Great."

"I hope you—"

"Forget it. I'm immortal," I said gruffly. I didn't mention that for some reason my knees felt weak. And nobody commented on what a dumb fool stunt I'd pulled.

Commander Aarons scowled over at me. "No," I heard him say. "I will talk to him later. Let the doctors have a look first."

A hand took my elbow roughly and guided me through the crowd. I winked at Jenny, hoping I looked self-confident.

There were two medical attendants with me. They hustled me into an elevator and we zipped inward five levels. I was in a daze. A doctor in a white coat poked at me, took a blood sample, urinalysis, skin sections—and then ordered me into a 'fresher.

I got a new set of standard ship work clothes when I came out, and a light supper. My time sense was all fouled up; it was early morning, ship's time, but my stomach thought it was lunch. And I felt like I was a million years old.

After that they left me alone.

Finally someone stuck his head in a door and motioned me into the next room. The doctor was in there, reading a chart.

"Young man," he said slowly, "you have given me and your parents and a lot of other people a great deal of trouble. That was an extremely foolish gesture to make. These past few days have been hard on all of us, but such heroics are not to be excused."

He looked at me sternly. "I imagine the Commander will have more to say to you. I hope he disciplines you well. By freak chance, you seem to have avoided getting a serious dosage of radiation. Your blood count is nearly normal. I expect it will reach equilibrium again within a few hours."

"I'm okay?"

"That is what I said, Your—"

There was a knock at the door. It opened and a bridge officer looked in. "Finished Doctor?"

"Nearly." He turned to me. "I want you to know that you came very close to killing yourself, young man. The background level out there is rising rapidly; it very nearly boiled you alive. Commander Aarons will make an example of you—"

"No doubt." I got up. The Doctor pressed his lips together into a thin line, then nodded reluctantly to the officer. We left.

"What now?" I said in the tube outside. "The Commander's office?"

"Nope. Mr. Jablons'."

"Why?"

"They don't let me in on their secrets. The Commander is there now. He sent me for you. If it was up to me, I'd have you thrashed, kid."

I didn't say anything more until we reached the electronics lab. There weren't any more convenient excuses. No dodges, no explanations. I had pulled off a dumb stunt and saved my neck only by smashing up *Roadhog*.

I slumped as I walked beside the bridge officer, my shoulders sagging forward. My conversation with Zak drifted through my head. *Self-knowledge is usually bad news.* Yeah. I thought back over what had been happening to me, the way one moment I'd act reasonably mature, and then the next minute I'd come on like some twelve-year-old. I hadn't dealt with Yuri, I hadn't straightened out my feelings about women, I hadn't even been able to take looking like a failure in Mr. Jablons' eyes . . .

Fuzzy thoughts floated by. The corridor seemed to ripple as I followed the bridge officer. I felt like some Earthside dope-o on mindwipe.

I took a deep breath and my head cleared a little. The bridge officer scowled at me. I tried to give him a smile with some bravado in it. It didn't work. We reached the electronics lab.

The Commander himself opened the door and waved the bridge officer away. He didn't look angry. In fact, he hardly saw me as I came in and closed the door. He was gazing off into space, thinking.

Dad and Mr. Jablons were sitting at one of the work benches. Dr. Kadin was working at a high-vacuum tank in the middle of the room. His hands were inserted in the waldoes and he was moving something inside the tank.

Dad looked up when I came in. "Ah, there you are, Mr. Lucky."

"Huh?"

"Look in the tank."

I walked over and looked through the glass. The Faraday cup was inside. Some of the sticky dust had been taken out with the waldo arms and scattered over a series of pyrex plates. The plates were spotted with green and blue chemicals and one of the plates was fixed under a viewing microscope.

"That contaminant you found inside the cup wasn't dust, Matt," my father said. "It is a colony of—well, something like spores. They are still active, as far as we can tell."

Dr. Kadin turned and looked at me. "Quite so. It would seem, young Mr. Bohles, that you have discovered life on Jupiter."

Chapter 14

Suddenly everybody in the room was smiling. Mr. Jablons laughed. "When they write this up in the history books, they'll have to record that blank look of yours, Matt."

I realized that my jaw was hanging open and quickly shut it. "Wha—How?"

"How did it get there?" Dr. Kadin said. "That is a puzzle. I imagine these spores—if that is indeed what they are—somehow traveled up through the Jovian atmosphere by riding along—'piggyback' I believe you say—on the electric fields produced by the turbulent storms."

Mr. Jablons slapped his knee. "I knew it would happen! Half an hour ago we didn't know if that dust was alive, and already a theory has raised its head."

Dr. Kadin ignored him. "You might have a look at them through the microscope," he said. "There are very interesting aspects."

I bent my head over the eyepiece of the microscope. Against a yellow smear I could see three brownish lumps. They looked like barbells with a maze of squiggly blue lines inside them. They weren't moving; the smear had killed them.

"Note the elongated structure," Dr. Kadin said at my ear. "Most unusual for such a small cell. Of course, these do not appear to be at all similar to Earthly cells in other particulars, so perhaps such a difference is not surprising."

"I don't get you," Dad said.

"I believe these organisms may use that shape to cause a separation of electrical charge in their bodies. Somehow, deep in the atmosphere, they shed charge. Then, when a storm blows them to the top of the cloud layer, they become attached to the complicated electrical field lines near the north pole."

"That's what brought them out to Satellite Fourteen?" I asked.

"I think so. It is the only mechanism I can imagine that would work."

"Why did the Faraday cup malfunction?" Commander Aarons asked. It was the first thing he had said since I arrived.

"Well, consider. When an electron strikes the cup it passes through the positive grid and strikes the negative plate. From there it passes down a wire and charges a capacitor. These spores—or whatever—are also charged; they will be trapped in the same manner. But they do not pass down the wire; only between grid and plate, eventually filling it up. They still retained some of their charge, though, and when they piled up high enough to connect the grid and the plate they shorted out the circuit." Dr. Kadin looked around, as if for approval.

"That could be why the Faraday cup failed, all right," Mr. Jablons said.

"I couldn't tell much from the microscope," I said. "Dr. Kadin, what are those cells like?"

"They *seem* to be carbon-based. They are not carbon dioxide absorbers, however, like terrestrial plants; perhaps they breathe methane. They have a thick cell wall and some structures I could not identify. Calling them spores is only a guess, really."

Commander Aarons shook his head. "You are certain these things couldn't have been left there by accident—just be something from the Can that was on the Bohles boy's gloves when he took it out?"

"No. They are like nothing I have ever seen."

"But what are they doing out there?" Dad said. "Why should organisms evolve that can be thrown clear above the atmosphere? If that bunch hadn't been trapped in Satellite Fourteen they could have gone all the way to the south pole, riding along on the magnetic fields."

"That may possibly be the point," Dr. Kadin said. "Perhaps these are spores and they were migrating."

"Migrating?" Dad said. "What for?"

"We know there are fewer storms near the poles. A point at the pole does not rotate like the rest of the planet;

the atmosphere above it is relatively still. It could be that only under those conditions can life survive in the Jovian atmosphere."

"I see," I murmured. "They were migrating to the other livable zone of the planet—the south pole."

"Perhaps, perhaps." Dr. Kadin waved his hands. "This is all quite preliminary. I am only advancing speculations, you understand."

"We can deal with theories later," Commander Aarons said. He smacked his fist into his palm. "The point is that we've found life—the real McCoy! If this doesn't make ISA sit up and take notice, nothing will."

"You think we might get to stay?" I said excitedly.

"We're back in the running, anyway. I am going to get Earthside on the line at once; this will make headlines on every continent, if I am any judge." He plucked at his moustache, smiling to himself. "Just wait until—"

"If you don't mind, gentlemen, before you leave I have a piece of data you might find interesting," Dad said. He got slowly to his feet, pausing for dramatic effect. I grinned. Dad could really play to the house, when he wanted to.

"I couldn't sleep while Matt was outside making an unintentional hero of himself; neither could his mother." I suddenly noticed bags under his eyes; he was tired. "I spent the time following up a project I've been meaning to get to for several weeks."

He picked a memory cube off the work table and inserted it in a viewscreen slot on the wall. The screen came to life.

At first I thought it was a bull's-eye—just a bunch of concentric circles with three large ellipses on the outside. Then I picked out one little dot on the rim of each curve and realized this was the orbit pattern of the Jovian moons; the bull's-eye at the center was Jupiter. As I watched, the dots moved. It was a speeded-up simulation.

"I had the computer plot out this history of the moons over the past month. All thirteen of the larger ones are here. You will notice that the outer moons do not move rapidly and have rather eccentric orbits. The outer three have never been visited by man; they appear to be smaller than the other moons and are probably asteroids captured when Jupiter was young."

"That is only a hypothesis," Dr. Kadin said.

"True, but a reasonable one." Dad paused again. "You have probably heard of the meteor swarms we have recently observed. They strike Jupiter near both the north and south poles. To do that requires an orbit that doesn't revolve in the same plane as Jupiter's equator, as the Can's does. It happens that the outer moons share this property."

"Ah," said Dr. Kadin.

"My reasoning wasn't this clear when I began. At the time I was simply interested in the orbits of the meteor swarms. Previously we had simply followed their orbits backwards until we could be sure they came from far out. I extended the calculation."

My father pressed a button and the screen flickered for a moment. The moon orbits were in yellow; now blue lines crawled away from Jupiter's circle and spiraled outward.

"This is a history of the meteor orbits, run backwards. This first swarm spreads out a little"—the blue lines fanned open—"and then bunches together again. That is unusual in itself. But notice where they bunch."

The lines focused together and intersected the eleventh Jovian moon.

"There isn't very much error in this work; we got good fixes on the swarm."

"Are you certain they had to strike J-11?" Dr. Kadin said. "It is a very small satellite."

"About twenty miles across, in fact. But the swarm had to hit it; I'm sure of that."

"Dad, 'hit' is the wrong word, isn't it? This display is running backwards. You mean the swarm started from J-11, don't you?"

"Right. Sloppy terminology. The program is still going through—watch this next swarm. The same pattern—spiraling out, bunching."

We watched the lines inch away from Jupiter. They came together just as they met the yellow dot that was J-12.

"Zap!" Mr. Jablons said. "I don't understand what's going on, but it looks beautiful."

"And strange," the Commander murmured.

"There's more," Dad said. "I'll speed it up."

Another family of lines wound outward, meeting at J-11. The next group was a little slower; they took their time, but they all ended up at J-12.

"Three earlier swarms show the same pattern."

"You have verified these calculations?" Dr. Kadin said.

"Yes."

"I am no astrophysicist," Commander Aarons said. "Maybe I am missing something in all this."

Dad shook his head. "I don't think you are, sir. This is something new to all of us. There isn't any handy explanation."

The room was quiet. Everyone was watching the screen. Blue lines crept out from Jupiter again.

"What could possibly cause it?" I said.

Dr. Kadin narrowed his eyes as he studied the lines.

"Let us go and find out," he said.

Chapter 15

I was on an emotional roller-coaster, of course. I had been for days, without really realizing it.

Soon Dr. Kadin fell into conversation about how to investigate J-11 and J-12. I sat and listened and slowly, slowly, the tension drained out of me. The room got very clear and bright. My arms and legs felt warm and tingly. The things people were saying were very interesting and I followed the conversation closely. But somehow I couldn't understand. The words were there, sure . . . but making the connections got harder . . . and harder. My eyes were sandy . . . and my eyelids kept creeping down.

I woke up the next morning. In my own bed.

I lay there for a while, feeling lazy and warm and letting my body drift. I thought about all that had happened. So much had come about by accident, the random collisions between people and events. Or it seemed random . . .

I mused about that for a while and then I got up. No point in lying around forever. Mom and Dad had already left for work. They left me a note on the newspad, telling me to take it easy and rest up. So I went for a walk, of course.

In the corridors outside, as I walked, I watched the faces. They were intent, but the mood was different from . . . was it only yesterday? People bustled along with fresh energy. A few recognized me. They stopped and slapped me on the back and said boisterous things. I smiled and told them it was just luck, nothing more, because that was the truth.

Zak was punching into a cubbyhole terminal near the comp center. He was frowning and typing as fast as he could. He looked over and saw me. His eyebrows shot up and he typed faster. In a minute he had cleared his program and gave up the terminal. "Matt-o!" He jumped up and came over to me. "I thought you'd be sipping champagne with the Commander."

"I'd settle for a bowl of cereal."

"I suppose you know you're the man on the white horse around here."

"Dumb luck."

"Don't fight it. People need heroes."

I grunted. Somehow I knew I wasn't going to like being the center of attention. "What's the update?" I asked.

"You don't know? The *Sagan* is going out to J-11. The crew's been selected. Aarons announced it an hour ago."

"Really? He's moving fast."

"Aarons wants to follow up your discovery, pronto. The way I figure it is, he doesn't want to give ISA time to react."

"Why not?"

"They'll advise extreme caution—you know bureaucracies. And some factions will say we're faking it, as a last-ditch measure to keep the Can alive."

"Jeee-sus."

"Welcome to the real world."

"So Aarons is going for J-11. What about probing Jupiter's atmosphere near the poles?"

Zak shrugged. "Most of the bio boys say that stuff you found comes from deep down—too deep for us to reach."

"Ummm. Hey, you said the crew's been selected?"

"Yeah. Aarons said—oh, I get it." He grinned. "You want to go."

"Sure. Wouldn't you?"

"Well, yeah, but . . ." He scowled. "My stock's not so high right now, anyway."

"Huh? Why not?"

Zak smiled wryly. "It's because of you, basically. You remember how Kadin got all fired up about those meteor swarm orbits?"

"Yeah."

"He assigned a couple of numerical specialists to comb back through the deep-memory storage and get all the records we had. That'll give us a history of the activity, Kadin thought. Maybe the early automated satellites—the post-Voyager craft—had picked up some odd stuff. So these numerical types went in and got everything out of storage, even the post-Voyager stuff, and started going through it, and . . ."

He paused significantly. A suspicion blossomed in my mind. "And *you* . . . Rebecca and Isaac . . ."

Zak nodded sourly.

"You said you had a foolproof place to store 'em." I couldn't help laughing.

"No need to cackle with glee," Zak muttered.

"And it had your ident code, right? So they knew right away whose it was."

"I never thought anybody'd go back into that old crap."

"Who nailed you?"

"Aarons called me in. Christ, I didn't think it would be that big a thing. I mean, with all that's going on—"

"What'd he say?"

"He gave me a long look and said something about improper use of facilities, and how I'd have a watchdog program on all my work from now on."

"You got off easy."

"Yeah, I guess. But I'm not any fair-haired boy, I can tell that. The comp center people keep laughing behind my back."

"Laughing?"

"Yeah. They seem to find some of what Rebecca and Isaac did, well, amusing."

"Ummm. Not, uh, exciting?"

"I guess not," Zak looked sour. I could tell he was more bothered by the laughter than the watch-dog program. I mean, to have your sexual fantasies taken as inept comedy . . .

I suppressed a smile and slapped him on the back. "Come on and have some breakfast."

"Don't you want to see the crew manifest for *Sagan*?"

"Oh yeah." Zak handed me a disposable printout. I scanned the names. Military people, mostly.

"Going to be some trip, all right," Zak mused.

"Yeah." Suddenly I wanted to go. To trace the swarms to their origin.

Zak could read my face. "Come on," he said. "Forget it. You may be the accidental savior, but you're still a kid."

We had breakfast. Zak didn't mind wolfing down a second; it helped console him. I was kind of quiet, thinking about J-11. Zak scooped up the tofu eggs and grumbled over his bad luck.

"You know," he said at last, "maybe I should've stuck to real life. Forget Rebecca and the business angle."

"Meaning what?"

"I should've put my effort into finding Lady X."

"You'll never learn, Zak."

Zak had a shift to work, so I wandered around for a while at loose ends. I wound up in the inner levels, near Hydroponics, and decided to put in some of my chore time there. Everybody has to do twenty hours a month of simple labor—recycling, cleaning filters, hauling stuff, anything that's so tedious that nobody wants to do it full time. Hydroponics work is mandatory for everybody, though, both because we have to maximize the food cultivated in the space allowed, and because it's psychologically good for you.

I checked in, got a work suit and found Mom. She was titrating a new fertilizing solution, checking its chemical balance. I left her to that and worked for a while putting patches on the duro tubing. I had to crawl through the close-packed, leafy tangle. In low g the plants grow two, maybe three times Earth norm. Tomatoes look like watermelons, and watermelons—well, you've got to see one to believe it. I went by the huge vat that holds Turkey Lurkey and peeked in. The big sweaty pale mass was perking right along, growing so fast you could almost see it swelling up. All the Can's meat comes from Turkey Lurkey. The chem wizards alter its taste with minute trace impurities, to make it seem like beef or fish or chicken. A lot of people Earthside thought Turkey Lurkey was here because eating live animals was wrong. Maybe that's a superior philosophical position, but the plain fact is that Turkey Lurkey is the only efficient way we could have any meat at all. There wasn't room for beef cattle or even chickens. Maybe the ethical issue was wrong anyway, because who was to say Turkey Lurkey wasn't conscious? Sure, it had a nervous system that made a nineteenth century telegraph line look like an IBM 9000, but what did that mean? Some neurophilosophers Earthside now think that consciousness may be a continuum, right down to plants. Who's to say? The plants aren't talking.

On our break I talked to Mom. As soon as I could, I brushed aside the talk about finding the stuff in the satellite. I mean, for some reason, praise from your own mother seems kind of obligatory. She'd say good things no matter what. And anyway, I wasn't interested in the past. I wanted in on the J-11 mission.

Mom didn't have any advice about that one, other than to suggest that I go see Commander Aarons about it. I knew that wouldn't work. So I talked about other things, and eventually we got around to the things Zak had said to me while I was out there, and about Earthside and my memories and all. I told Mom how I felt. It wasn't easy.

"Yes, I remember Dr. Matonin mentioning that to me," Mom said.

"Huh? When?"

"Oh, years ago."

"How'd *she* know?"

"Why, they have a profile on everyone."

"Why'd she never say anything to *me* about it?"

"I suppose she thought it wouldn't do any good."

"She told *you*."

"Only to make me more aware of the problem. We weren't gossiping behind your back, Matt."

"What was the good Doctor's therapy?" I asked dryly.

Mom smiled. "No therapy. There's a limit to what anyone else can do about these things, Matt."

"Right," I muttered gruffly. "Damned right."

Something in that conversation crystallized my thoughts. I felt a slow, sullen anger building up inside me. I went over to the storage shed and threw bags of fertilizer onto the slideways. Hefting them up and dumping them down gave my muscles a chance to do my thinking for me. Long ago I'd learned that when I felt this way, a workout was the best solution. Fertilizer bags can't fight back.

And as I sweated and grunted it all started to make sense. Doctor Matonin and her mother-henning. Those dumb Socials. Yuri's father, making his son look like a fool by acting out some antique dream of Earthside. They were all putting blinders on us, shaping us with their dimly remembered ideas about growing up.

I thought about Jenny. The only time we had really said anything worth a damn to each other was on *Roadhog*. Outside the Can. On our own. Away from all the eyes and ever-ready advice. Away from the rules and guidelines and the whole goddamn suffocating adult world.

I had learned something out there in the long, black hours on *Roadhog*. I would have seen it eventually, I knew, if I'd just kept on with the orbital missions. My crazy run to get the Faraday cup had just speeded up the process. Getting outside the Can gave you a perspective. It was a big help to look back on your whole life and see it stuffed into a tin box, literally see it for the tight little world it was. Because otherwise, you'd buy the official Can point of view. You'd go along. And you'd never really grow up. You'd turn into a Zak, wiseassing way through life. Or a Yuri, crippled by a blockhead parent. That was the danger of compression, of packing people so close together they *had* to get along. In those circumstances, everybody had to back down, live life according to the concensus rules.

That might be okay if you were already an adult. You had your own internal gyroscope then. You knew where you were headed. But to grow up you had to take *risks*. That was the key. You had to do what seemed right to *you*, not right to the majority.

To stop being a kid you had to have the right to be wrong. And that was what the Can couldn't tolerate. So the quiet, steady pressure was on. Don't step out of line. Don't let yourself go. Don't let passion or anger sweep you away.

Well, screw that. I thought back over the last month and I could see how I'd been acting. One minute I was the cooperative, likable Matt, and the next I was filled with doubts, worries. Typical adolescent stuff. But my dopey ride out to get that Faraday cup had changed something inside me now. I had risked something—my life—and those long dark hours arcing back to the Can had changed me. Right, it had been a stupid gamble. So what? The point was, I took it. I did something for *me*, not for the Jupiter Project. It wasn't like the hike I took on Ganymede to get the air bottles. I did that because Yuri challenged me. Going for the Faraday cup was for *me*, not for the Can.

So I made a promise to myself. Growing up was painful, sure. But I was going to do it. I was going to make Matt Bohles the way *he* wanted to be. I was going to face risks—risks of all kinds. When the time came, I was going to change. If you want to grow, you have to gamble.

I slaved away for two more hours harvesting bean sprouts. It's wet work. The vaporizers pump out clouds of big, wobbly bubbles that take forever to fall in the low g. They blow into the sprout paddies, cloudy with nutrients. You get soaked. You can inhale one through your nostrils if you don't watch it.

I was loading bags of sprouts onto the conveyor when

I noticed the guy who was delivering the recycled bags. It was Yuri.

He looked at me for a long moment. I knew I could turn away and wade back into the paddies. He wouldn't follow me, particularly since he didn't have hip boots on. But that wasn't the right way to handle it.

I walked over to him, keeping my hands relaxed at my sides. "Sorry about that," I said.

He grimaced, "I think you will soon be more than sorry."

"Doesn't seem likely."

"Your luck will not carry you forever."

"You have a point." He started to turn away. "Look, Yuri, there's something I want to ask you. Why have you been riding me?"

He halted. A puzzled look crossed his face. "I . . . I had to, Bohles. You were ahead of me."

"So?"

"I . . . my talents are not the same as yours, but . . . the Laboratory rewards your . . . sort . . . more than mine."

"So what? Who says you have to win on *their* terms?"

Yuri looked at me blankly. "We are . . . not alike. I have different . . . ideas about . . ."

"It's your father, isn't it? He's been pushing you."

"It must be obvious even to you that our families are different. My father has strong ideas . . ."

"Look, he made you dress up in that—"

Yuri scowled and I saw that I had gone too far. He didn't want to remember that.

"Garbage, Bohles, garbage. If you can't take the competition, get out."

"That's not what I meant. You and me could—"

"Don't give me any goddam breaks, Bohles," Yuri snapped, and marched away.

I shrugged. Some games you can't win. some gambles you lose.

I worked off my aggression on the bean sprouts. That tired me out, but it didn't stop me from thinking about J-11.

I went out for a drink that evening, with Jenny. We talked about the Jovian life-form, and the flood of questions that needed answering. The bio types were doing flip-flops, changing theories faster than they changed their underwear.

The saga of Rebecca and Isaac was by now common scuttlebutt, too, so I gave in to Jenny's questions and told her about it. Now that I thought about the whole thing, it was more funny than embarrassing.

And through it all, I felt an odd hovering presence between Jenny and me. We edged toward the subject slowly, but each of us sensed that the other wanted to talk, talk the way we had before. I found myself agreeing with her. "I've felt it, too," I said quietly. "They don't want us to get emotionally involved, I guess. So, almost without thinking about it, they've set up the Can . . ."

Jenny finished it for me. "For their age group, not ours."

"Yeah."

"A programmed world."

"And in a way, they're right," I said. "This *is* a damned dangerous place. Ishi . . ." My voice trailed off.

Jenny said, "When you add all that, on top of all the crap separating men and women already . . ."

"Yeah. The distrust. The anger."

"And the just plain awkwardness. But we've got to overcome it."

"How?"

"By being our*selves*," Jenny said.

"It's hard to be yourself when you're in a fishbowl."

"You mean when everybody's watching."

"Right."

"You know . . ." She smiled a quiet, mischievous smile that I had seen a few times and liked a lot. "It *is* hard to get any privacy around here. But I know a place."

"Where?"

"I do some of my chore time in the infirmary. There's a reserve room, kept stocked with med stations and beds, in case of a major accident. Not many people even know it's there, we use it so seldom." She looked at me sideways and bit her lip. A hesitant turn crept into her smile.

"We might get caught."

"I suppose so."

I felt an odd electric tingling. A quickening, nervous energy.

To grow, gamble.

What can you say about it? That all the thousands of hours you spent trying to imagine it never prepared you for the real thing. That it really is different from anything else. And that yet in a way it's like a lot of other things, physical and emotional, all merged and heightened and more intense. You're clumsy, sure. But there's something about it that takes you out of yourself and into some other place. And it takes you into the person you're with.

There's all that, sure. But mostly it's a huge, gaudy kind of fun.

When Jenny and I left the infirmary I felt emotions that were new to me. Love, maybe; it's hard to tell. I know the things you feel when you're an adolescent are going to change with time, the way everybody and everything does—but still, the warm aura that surrounded us was real, not some kid's delusion. I wasn't just feeling the "release of tension" the manuals tell you about. It was more like Jenny and I had been to a place that you can't get to without something very special happening. Exactly what all that meant, we'd find out in time. For now, it was enough to have been there.

As we ambled along the dimly lit nighttime corridors, I said, "Y'know, it's funny, how some things are right in front of you and still you don't see them."

"Ummm. Such as?"

"I had to be jolted into paying attention. Into taking my nose off the grindstone."

"Oh?" Jenny arched her eyebrows.

"That stunt of mine, flying out to Satellite Fourteen. The regular Matt Bohles wouldn't have done that."

"Probably not."

"I guess all this—yeah, including my interest in you—started with Ishi."

She looked at me. "How?"

"Well, I started thinking of these things, you know."

"But not about me in particular?"

"Well, no, not at first."

Jenny was looking at me in a funny way. "You mean, it was because Ishi died? Not because of something he said?"

"No, because he died. It . . . I don't know, everything seemed different after that."

"Yes," she said softly, "it was."

The next day I did more chore work, lugging sacks of compost. It was the only kind of thing I felt like doing. Halfway through the morning I got a comm call. It was Commander Aarons' office. They wanted me at a meeting in one hour. I went back to work and mulled it over. Probably a more thorough debriefing of my Satellite Fourteen run, I guessed. ISA would want them to dot all the i's and cross all the t's.

When I got there, all changed into a new suit, there wasn't anybody I'd expected. No Dr. Kadin, no Mr. Jablons. Commander Aarons' secretary—a guy I knew from the squash ladder—made me sit and wait. I could hear some loud talking from the inner office; the sealite partitions can only muffle so much. I couldn't make out who was talking.

A light flashed on the secretary's console. He told me to go on in.

Sitting in a chair across from the Commander's desk was Yuri's father.

"I thought you might be interested in Dr. Sagdaeff's complaint. He has filed it against you," Aarons said.

Dr. Sagdaeff said stiffly, "I see no reason why he should be here. This is a disciplinary matter—"

"Oh, it's more than that."

I began, "Look, sir, I'd just as soon avoid—"

"No, sit down," Aarons said. "This is indeed more than a disciplinary matter. State your case, Dr. Sagdaeff."

Yuri's father frowned and glanced at me. "Briefly, we all know what this boy did to Yuri. Assault, that is the term, I believe. And the boy risked his own life, and destroyed valuable equipment, in a foolhardy stunt."

"Hey, there—"

Aarons silenced me with a raised palm. Yuri's father went on, "However, you are certainly aware that the feeling in the Laboratory runs strongly in favor of this boy. He was, I'll admit, very fortunate. But that does not erase the offense against my son."

"Agreed." Commander Aarons made a steeple of his fingers and peered at them.

"And it is not a trivial offense. Yuri could have been seriously hurt."

"Perhaps."

"What is more, my son, by trying to stop this boy, has been made to look like the villain. It appears to me that, even beyond the issue of punishment for the assault, one should consider the harm to my son's prestige among his co-workers."

I was seething, but I kept my trap shut. Commander Aarons tapped on his desk top with a pen. "And so . . . ?"

"I ask that, to compensate my son, he be included in the crew which goes to investigate the J-11."

"*What*?" I cried. "What can *he* do that—"

"Quiet." Commander Aarons shifted forward, putting his elbows on his desk and peering at Dr. Sagdaeff. "Of course, none of this is a coincidence. I am sure you have already learned, Dr. Sagdaeff, that one of the *Sagan* crew has been injured. A deep cut, from a loading accident. She must be replaced."

Yuri's father smiled slightly and nodded.

Aarons glowered. He seemed to get larger. "But to come to me with this case—incredible, sir, incredible. I am not in the business of insuring your son's reputation. I am *not* a settler of petty disputes. And I will *not* be pushed into making assignments on a political basis."

Yuri's father twisted his mouth. "I hope you realize what harm this decision can do to your own position, eh? There are those in ISA who believe you have been altogether too arbitrary already in your policies. I would expect—"

Aarons stood up. "That, sir, is too much. Your faction is well known to me. I hear about your maneuverings constantly. But *you* do not have to insure the safety of this Laboratory. *Your* only obligation is to complain."

"I think that is totally unfair—"

"To hell with your idea of fairness."

"—and your own attitude will be well documented, I assure—"

"Your son is inexperienced at long flights outside the Can. He is unqualified," Commander Aarons said stiffly.

"No more so than others. I feel he is owed—"

"I will not have you strong-arming me with your ISA connections. Out!"

"What?" Dr. Sagdaeff looked surprised. "You cannot insult a senior member of the staff by ordering him to—"

"Out! Or do I have to assist you to the door?"

Yuri's father froze for a moment, reassessing the situation. It obviously hadn't gone the way he thought it would. "I hope you realize—"

"Out!"

Dr. Sagdaeff stood slowly and turned toward the door.

"Oh, yes," Aarons said, a little of the steam leaving his voice, "I suppose I do owe you the favor of being the first to hear the announcement, Dr. Sagdaeff. Seeing as how you are a senior member of the staff and all that." He smiled without mirth. "I had chosen the replacement before you even came to see me. I made the decision before you could try to put your political spin on it, you see. What *Sagan* needs is somebody with experience on shuttle-type craft."

He pointed at me. "And there he is."

Chapter 16

It took two more days to outfit the *Sagan* for an extra-long flight. I spent most of the time working with Mr. Jablons on the Faraday cups. The biologists were concentrating on the spores themselves so much, nobody had taken the time to figure out how we found them in the first place.

After some tinkering, we figured out why the cup on Satellite Seventeen had cleared up after it had left the region above the poles. It turned out that the spores had their charge bled away after a few hours of contact with the grid and plate. Simple electrical conduction. When their charge vanished they were no longer attracted to the grid, so they gradually drifted out and away into space.

But the biologists had the limelight. Everybody wanted details and everybody had a half-baked theory. Dr. Kadin held a seminar that packed the auditorium. Earth kept the laser comm net saturated with questions, and they televised Dr. Kadin's talk for prime-time showing Earthside.

In the question session afterward, somebody asked why the older cup I had replaced hadn't shorted out, too. I had to admit I didn't know. Maybe the cups didn't have exactly identical electrical characteristics. Or maybe only a few of the storms carried spores. I had no idea. As the scientists say when they want to wriggle out from under, that aspect of the problem will be left for future research.

I trained for my job. We were taking along a shuttlecraft that had been in storage. It was outfitted with better detectors and special equipment, hydraulics and electron-beam cutters and omnisensors. We would carry it out on the hull of the *Sagan*. I was to be the pilot. I named it *Roadhog*. Sentimental, I guess.

There was a big, noisy crowd saying good-bye at the main lock. Somebody was taking 3D scans for Earthside media hype. I said good-bye solemnly to my mother and waved at friends. Zak thumped me on the back, grinning.

"Hold the fort," I said. I grabbed Jenny and gave her a long kiss that unfocused her eyes. I shook hands in a manly, exaggerated way with Zak. Then I lugged my gear out to the *Sagan*.

It took three days to reach J-11. We maneuvered into a parallel orbit thirty klicks away from it and the scientists got busy peering at it in the optical, infrared, UV, and beyond. J-11 was an unappetizing lump of rock, a flying mountain. Jagged peaks caught the sunlight and pooled the low spots in shadow. The whole thing was barely thirty klicks across at its longest dimension. There were no snowdrifts or clumps of ice clinging in dark corners, just

cratered granite-gray rock. That suggested it had not con-
densed out of the primordial soup around Jupiter. It was
probably a captured asteroid, tugged into orbit by tidal
forces long ago.

We saw no swarms. Nothing on J-11 moved. So the
next step was a close reconnaissance—and I got to go.

I suited up and went out onto the hull to check out
Roadhog. Maybe it should have been *Roadhog II,* but that
would've been pretentious. I clumped around in magnetic
boots. Commander Aarons came out to look things over. I
repped and verified all systems. He waved to the exploration party of eight that I was to ferry over. They climbed
on and belted in.

This was where *Roadhog* was essential. We couldn't
risk taking the *Sagan* in close to J-11; any small error in
jockeying around could smash the ship into a peak. In the
Roadhog a small party could slip into the fissures and get a
good look if they needed to.

Lt. Sharma was in charge. His orders were to nose
around and report back. The civilian head of the group
was my father; one of his jobs, I was sure, would be
keeping an eye on me. After all, I was the kid who
disobeyed direct orders and stole a shuttle.

We took our time crossing the thirty kilometers. Jenny
and I had fitted extra seats on *Roadhog* back at the Can
and now the exploration party was belted into them behind me. What with equipment lashed to every available
pipe and strut, we looked like a gypsy wagon.

Jupiter hung off to the left. This far out it didn't fill
the sky anymore; its orange bands were creamy and
smooth, with no detail, and Ganymede was a frozen silver
dot at its side. The scenery hadn't really changed that
much, considering that we were twenty-two million kilometers from the Can.

J-11 was tumbling slightly and I had to correct several
times before we were hanging steady over one spot on its
surface. I nudged us in slowly, watching the shadows
below shift as the tiny moon rotated in the sunlight.

Nobody said anything; most of them were busy taking
pictures and watching their meters. After I fixed our rela-

tive position there wasn't much to do; J-11's gravity was so weak it would take years to draw us in.

After several minutes I said, "Dad?"

"Yes, son?"

"See that crater down there? The big one, between the twin peaks?"

"Ummmm. Yes. What about it?"

"For a minute there I thought I saw a bright flash, like metal reflecting the sun, right down at the bottom."

"I can't see the bottom."

"It's in shadow now. The rock must be dark there, anyway; I couldn't see anything even when the sunlight was slanting down into it."

"Let's go in closer," one of the other men said. I looked at Lt. Sharma, who was sitting next to me. "Go ahead," he said.

I nudged the *Roadhog* nearer. The crater grew. I was busy watching our trajectory and didn't look up until someone yelled "Hey! There's a hole in it."

He was right. The "crater" was a bottomless pit, several miles across. Where you would expect to see a flat floor there was nothing, just blackness. Utter, eerie blackness.

There was a lot of chatter over suit radio. I tuned it out and concentrated on my piloting. Every few minutes Lt. Sharma would confer with the Commander and obtain permission to go in closer. One of the men behind me was running a portable television camera so they could follow what as happening back on the *Sagan*.

The hole remained black. We went in closer. One kilometer, then a half, then four hundred yards. One of the scientists checked the radiation level and found nothing more than the usual background count. I aimed the *Roadhog*'s headlights off to the side and got back a few sparkling reflections from the distant walls. The sides of the pit seemed to be fused and melted here and there.

Lieutenant Sharma asked for permission to go into the pit. The Commander argued a little and then granted it.

I took her down. The yawning crater swallowed us in shadow.

The radio was quiet now. No one had anything more to say. Just before we went in I looked to the side and saw the rim of the crater rise up. Then it was blotted out by the edge of the pit. Behind us the *Sagan* jockeyed to stay within our line of sight; otherwise, we would lose radio contact.

There still wasn't much to see. The pit walls were far away and most of the rock could have passed for coal; it was *dark*.

"Lieutenant! I am registering an increased magnetic field," one of the men behind me said.

"What's that?" my father asked, pointing. I turned the craft to bring the headlights toward the walls of the pit. A dim coppery ribbon lined the wall. I rotated the *Roadhog*. The band formed a thin ring completely around the pit. We were passing through the center of the ring.

"What is it?"

"Looks like metal."

"Impossible."

"Quiet," said Lieutenant Sharma, and spoke to the Commander.

I didn't slacken our speed. Another ring came into view. As we passed through it I thought it looked a little closer to the shuttle. I wondered how such a natural formation could come about. Something to do with the evolution of the asteroid belt? Veins of metal? The rings were at least half a kilometer in diameter, larger than the diameter of the Can.

We came to another. And another. They were getting closer together. Smaller, too. The pit was narrowing.

"Something is reflecting light ahead," Lieutenant Sharma said, breaking a long silence. His voice was a dry rasp.

I slowed the shuttle. It was hard to make out any detail. We coasted through a chain of rings, each a little smaller than the last. I was beginning to get a creepy feeling.

Something metallic lay ahead; it looked like the same mottled coppery stuff as in the rings. I brought us up to it slowly, ignoring the radio conversation. It wasn't until we were quite close that I saw that the pit had ended; the metal object was sitting on a wall of dry rock.

We hung about a hundred meters away from the wall. The coppery object was a hemisphere without any visible markings, about ten meters across.

I glanced at Lieutenant Sharma. He was looking off the side, squinting. He pointed toward the walls of the pit. "That way," he said.

I was more interested in the metal dome, but I followed orders. We coasted along parallel to the pit floor. Then I saw a blotch ahead that resolved into a rectangle of white.

"Hey!" someone said.

Suddenly the pit floor was gone. I looked down and saw nothing but blackness. There was an opening below us. Lieutenant Sharma pointed at it and nodded to me. I took the *Roadhog* into the hole, fumbling nervously with the attitude jets.

The walls in this hole didn't narrow. There was a clearance of about twenty meters. A moment passed before I realized that walls existed only on two sides, the left and right. In the other directions there was only darkness.

What we had thought was the floor of the pit was only something blocking it, like a cork that doesn't fill the neck of a bottle. Now we were inching around the cork.

Something loomed ahead, and I slowed the shuttle down.

"Looks like a pipe," someone said.

"Yes, it does," my father answered. "About five meters in diameter. It comes out of the wall on the right."

"And connects into the rock on the left," Lieutenant Sharma said. He pressed his lips together as he studied it.

I inched us around the pipe. In the shuttle's pale headlights it looked flexible. Where it joined the wall there were folds in the material. Beyond this pipe we could see others, evenly spaced.

"Let's go back," Lieutenant Sharma said. "I want to have a look at that white thing."

There was some argument, but I was taking orders only from the Lieutenant. Eagerly I backed us out, into the clear. The enormity of this thing was just starting to hit me.

When we came out I steered us toward the white rectangle I had noticed before. It was set into the wall of the pit, flush with the rock and measured about a hundred meters on a side.

There were odd-shaped openings in it, some with curlicues of metal standing beside them. I found it hard to get my bearings as we approached. Piloting in that vast inky dark was unnerving.

I stopped about ten meters from the face of the thing, and Lieutenant Sharma turned around and pointed out two men to go with him. They cast off together and coasted over, using their suit jets. Not until they had touched down on the surface of the thing did I recognize one of them as my father.

There was an eerie stillness about the place. No one talked. They examined the surface for a few minutes. Then my father said it seemed like aluminum but was stronger. They conferred about their next move and decided to go into one of the openings.

Something that looked like an abstract metal sculpture was set in next to the nearest opening. They carefully clipped a line to it. Then the Lieutenant disappeared from sight over the edge of the hole. The opening was as big as the *Roadhog* and seemed to have smooth sides. My father snaked in after the Lieutenant, following the line. The third man hung at the edge, looking down and holding a hand flashlight for illumination.

We waited. As soon as Dad and the Lieutenant were out of sight we lost radio contact with them. The other men started talking, but I ignored them. I was busy watching the mouth of the opening and looking for anything coming at us from the darkness all around. Nothing moved. A distant circle framed glowing stars; that was the mouth of the pit. We must have come seven or eight kilometers into J-11, at least.

Minutes crawled by. It was spooky, sitting there in nearly total darkness. It seemed as though my father had been gone a long time. What could they be doing in there? I wondered if Commander Aarons knew how long they had been in. Maybe he hadn't noticed—

The man at the edge waved to someone below. A moment later my father coasted out, holding the line. The Lieutenant followed. They touched helmets and gestured back at the opening.

After a moment Lt. Sharma looked our way and said over radio, "Why don't three more come down. I'm sure you all have measurements to make."

I didn't wait for the three to be picked. I swarmed over the side and flew across on jets. The white metal rang faintly under my boots as I landed. For a few minutes I helped set up cameras and other gear. Then I drew Dad aside.

"How long are we going to be here, Dad?" I said. "I'd like to have a look inside."

"Not long enough. I don't want people haphazardly wandering around, anyway. Could be dangerous."

I looked around at the warped and tangled fingers of metal. I shivered. Standing here among them I felt a cold strangeness.

"Well, okay. But—who were they?"

"The people who built this?" He shook his head. "No way to tell. From the size of the doorways inside—if that is what they are—I would say they were large, at least twice as tall as we are."

"They couldn't be from Jupiter?"

"Not likely. Jupiter is a thick atmosphere over an even thicker ocean. There are no continents down there, no land at all. Could a fish discover fire—or build a rocket?"

"What other possibilities are there? There wasn't any life on Mars, or even Ganymede."

"They weren't from this system, Matt. I just saw some evidence to support that when I was inside. There is a—well, I can only guess that it's a display board, but I don't know how it works. It came to life when I entered the room. It seems to be a holographic three-dimensional project of the nearby stars, with Sol at the center.

"About five light-years away, as nearly as I can estimate, there is a green object. It's at a point just beyond the Centauri system, where I know there isn't any star. Besides, the green dot lies on a thin blue line that runs inward from the edge of the projection. The blue line stops here—at Sol. Something tells me the blue is a chartered course for a star ship and that green dot is the ship."

"Five light-years out. Maybe someone was here before the Can was constructed and left."

Dad smiled. "I think we would have noticed something. We've had probes around Jupiter for fifty years."

"Then they're not going away? They're . . . coming?"

"That's my guess. It fits the rest."

"What rest?"

"This tunnel. Those metal rings we saw reminded me of our ion engines. I'll bet they are superconducting magnets. The tunnel is a giant induction accelerator."

I blinked. "Huh? For what?"

"The meteoroid swarms. Look at that thing," he said, pointing off into the gloom at the huge rock "cork" we had found blocking the tunnel. "I have a hunch that will be the next swarm we see. Something is pumped into it through those pipes, then it's broken up and accelerated down this tube. A giant shotgun."

"Aimed at the poles of Jupiter," I said.

"Yes . . ." I could see Dad was thinking. He looked at some of the oddly twisted metal around us and frowned. Whatever the metal was, it had iron in it; our magnetic boots held. "You know, Matt," he said at last, "I'm not a believer in coincidence. The storms, the meteor swarms, suddenly you found life spiraling out of the atmosphere on electric field lines—it all happened at once."

"I wonder what we would find if we opened that rock cork in the tunnel," I said thoughtfully.

"What do you mean?"

"Could somebody be, well *seeding* Jupiter? Getting it ready for whatever is in that star ship?"

"Seed it for what?"

"I don't know. To produce food? Maybe for a fish that can build star ships?" I grinned.

"That's a big project. Jupiter has millions of times the life-supporting volume Earth does."

"Size won't stop men; I don't see why it should stop

anything else that can think. In fifty years we might be wrapping a sheet around Ganymede's atmosphere to keep the oxygen in and make a better greenhouse out of it. Given time maybe we can do something with Jupiter, too—if somebody doesn't beat us to the property first."

Dad gingerly touched one of the metal things. "Perhaps . . . perhaps. We're all going to be cooking up theories about this place, and no one will know the right answer until that green dot gets here."

"You and I will be around to see it happen, Dad," I said. "ISA can't ship me Earthside now."

"Not without a fight from me, and the commander too, I expect." He waved to the other men. "Better pack up!" he called. "We ought to bring the whole expedition down and set up a base at the edge of the crater. We want to do this carefully."

He moved over to talk to the rest. I looked back at the beckoning circle at the end of the tunnel. The *Sagan* was a sharp bright point framed by Jupiter's smoky bands.

Jupiter changes constantly. Her bands are an elaborate waltz of white streamers, crimson splotches, lacy brown filaments. The Red Spot seethes and churns. I was going to see a lot of the bands; I might spend my whole life out here.

Somebody has to be around when the owners of J-11 return. There'll be a whole colony out here by then, waiting. Zak would stay, probably, despite his fatalism. Mom and Dad, yes—it was in their blood.

Jenny, too—and what that meant for me I couldn't say. Not yet.

Yuri might even stay. Well, I'd handle that too.

That chilling knot of fear in me was gone now, burned away. I'd been carrying that fear since I was a kid. If it ever came back I could recognize it, overcome it. A lot of problems are like that—they wither away if you look at them straight on, unflinching. To grow, gamble. Self-knowledge isn't always bad news, after all.

It felt good inside to know that. Ultimately, there isn't anything *worth* fearing.

The Lab people knew that. They had come this immense distance across the ocean of space, risking everything, living in a cramped tin can—all for the sake of knowledge, to stick their noses into things, to see what makes the universe tick. It's a human thing to do. Without it we'd bore ourselves to death.

I couldn't predict the future, but I did know one thing: I wasn't going to get bored.

"Matt!" my father called. "We're loading up."

I freed my magnetic anchors and went to help.

ABOUT THE AUTHOR

GREGORY BENFORD is the author of several acclaimed novels, including *Tides of Light, Great Sky River, Heart of the Comet* (with David Brin), *In the Ocean of Night, Across the Sea of Suns, Against Infinity,* and *Timescape,* which won the Nebula Award, the British Science Fiction Award, the John W. Campbell Memorial Award, and the Australian Ditmar Award. Dr. Benford, a Woodrow Wilson Fellow, is a professor of physics at the University of California, Irvine. He and his wife live in Laguna Beach.

The groundbreaking novels of
GREGORY BENFORD

☐ **In the Ocean of Night** (26578-4 • $3.95/$4.95 in Canada) From deepest space, a mystery emerges as vast as the limitless sea of stars. This is one man's encounter with that mystery. *The Magazine of Fantasy and Science Fiction* called this "A major novel."

☐ **Across the Sea of Suns** (28211-5 • $4.50/$5.50 in Canada) Technology has created a new age of enlightenment for humanity. As earth falls prey to attack, from the far reaches of space comes an alien message of astounding importance, revealing great wonders and terrifying danger.

☐ **Great Sky River** (27318-3 • $4.95/$5.95 in Canada) The story of the last surviving humans, their struggle to survive against a mechanical alien civilization, and the unexpected fate that awaits them.

☐ **Tides of Light** (28214-X • $4.50/$5.50 in Canada) Killeen and his band gain an unexpected ally in their battle for survival, and make an unexpected contribution to the new order of life developing at the galactic center.

☐ **Heart of the Comet** (with David Brin) (25839-7 • $4.95/$5.95 in Canada) chronicles the daring mission to the heart of Halley's Comet by a team of brilliant—and very human—scientists. *The San Diego Union* called it "Better than *Dune*...a breathtaking effort from two of science fiction's brightest stars."

☐ **If the Stars Are Gods** (with Gordun Eklund) (27642-5 • $3.95/$4.95 in Canada) Scientist Bradley Reynolds must decode a mysterious signal hinting at intelligent life amid the gasses of Jupiter, and must ultimately make a challenging journey to find his answers.

☐ **The Jupiter Project** (28631-5 • $4.50/$5.50 in Canada) When the crew of the Jovian Orbital Laboratory learns that non-essential personnel—most of whom have grown up on the station—are to be relocated to Earth, many decide instead to move to Jupiter, discovering things more alien than anything they might have found on humanity's home world.